WHAT DID YOU DO
FOR A LIVING, DADDY?

Gordon C. Krantz

"Daddy" would be, by now,
more appropriately
"Grandpa" or even
"Great Grandpa."

First written a decade ago,
and re-edited in 2009,
this book is a delayed attempt
to address the problem
that my kids had had
in school, many years past.
See the opening paragraphs.

Oh yes, that cover.
Well, it was a checkered career.

ISBN # 978-0-578-01552-1

TABLE OF CONTENTS

Chapter   **page**

WHAT DID YOU DO FOR A LIVING, DADDY?
Gordon C. Krantz

INTRODUCTION

The problems with my having had a checkered career, holding jobs with vague or obscure titles, hit the kids hardest. They went to school and the day came when each student was supposed to go home and report back what their fathers did for a living. (That was in the 1950s, when all fathers worked and all mothers were homemakers.)

Well, my kids went home and dutifully asked me what I did. Then they went back and reported, "He told me what he did for a half hour, but I still don't know what he does." So much for concise communication.

This essay is an attempt to answer the question again, now that the kids are old enough to read (*Their* kids are old enough to read!). Please bear with a bit of rambling, because the road is 80+ years long and it winds over the landscape, sometimes with multiple tracks.

My passport says that I'm a psychologist. And that's true enough in its way. I was for many years first a Certified Psychologist and later a Licensed Consulting Psychologist and still have a lifetime license as School Psychologist II, but those are state administrative classifications that bear little upon what I really did for a living. The title allowed me to do what I wanted to do and it still is a useful way to get through Immigration and Customs.

However, as you will see, mostly I had a hard time explaining what I did for the good reason that my jobs were often deliberately vaguely defined and titled.

In the modern world that's not remarkable; in the old world of the 1950s to 1980s, it was. In those days you took a job with the expectation that it would be your career. If you were a carpenter you retired as a carpenter. Now kids probably are not asked what their fathers do for a living. The answers might be awkward. And changing careers is normal.

NOTE: What I did for real, in contrast to what I did for a living, is not described here. In real life I was a husband, father, active church member and aspiring Christian, iconoclast, mediocre fisherman, tinkerer, and frustrated idler.

What I did for a living interfered with most of those roles. Not, I hope, too much.

ANOTHER NOTE: This is more of an archive than a fascinating memoir. Be patient. Life really is that complicated. And if I don't toot my own horn, who will?

FIRST FARM
1930s to 1942

I was born to farming. Well, not really, because I was born in an upstairs bedroom in Red Wing, to a carpenter's family. But when I was 3-1/2 years old we moved to a 40-acre farm in Isanti County: ten miles northwest of Cambridge and 4 miles southwest of Stanchfield, in east central Minnesota.

The seven of us took on the Great Depression, which struck less than 3 years after we moved, on 40 acres of peat and sand. We lived. Brother Stan took to the rails for a while, inaugurating his life of roaming, and that made one less mouth to feed. But also one less worker. Before and after his riding the rails (kids, that's what we called being a hobo) Stan worked for farmers a few miles away and that was small but welcome income. In later years Stan amplified this in his mind to the effect that he was the support of the family -- and to that extent, he was. But he was not the sole or even major support because the rest of us worked the farm on a non-cash basis.

We milked our seven cows, raised our half dozen hogs, drove our team of small horses, and raised potatoes like everyone around us. OK, so I didn't do much work at first. But by the time I was ten years old and we were moving to another farm I was doing what I thought of as my share of work.

My earliest memory of work is that of picking potatoes. In our neighborhood the economy was so potato-dependent that the schools had "potato vacation" just before freeze-up in the fall. I see myself joining the rest of the family at about age 5 or 6, walking behind Dad as he dug (by hand, with a fork) the hills of potatoes, picking up the spuds and putting them in my pail. In deference to my age my pail was a gallon syrup pail. The others used 2-gallon galvanized pails.

3

Potatoes were harvested after the vines were killed by the frost and before the ground froze. To store them we cleared a space of about 6 feet across and piled the potatoes about 3 feet high in a cone. Then we'd lay the dead vines over them and cover the whole with dirt. Preserved that way they'd escape freezing until well into December. We had limited heated storage space on our farm. We did have a small root cellar, a semi-pit structure on a side field, covered with sod and with a small door, but that couldn't hold the whole harvest. As opportunity presented we'd break into the mounds in the fields and haul potatoes in the wagon to Cambridge to sell them. At least, Dad did. As the youngest I didn't get into the big city more than once or twice a year.

If potatoes froze in the field all was not lost. We had one of those big cast-iron kettles suspended in the yard and frozen or otherwise bad potatoes were boiled there for the pigs. I can still smell the brew, not really offensive but not something that would make you hungry.

My second early memory is that of the breaking plow. Yes, I did walk behind a breaking plow. That's a two-horse plow with a knife coulter (a sharp vertical blade to cut the sod) and two curved handles. You knotted the reins, looped them over one shoulder, and steered the plow by its handles. I must have been nearly ten then and probably didn't do much plowing, but I can honestly claim to have broken sod that had never been plowed. We were expanding a field across what had been a marshy vacant strip.

But I was younger when I had my first "foreign" adventure. About 4 ½ or 5. I'd heard of the Rum River, a branch of the Mississippi that ran some five miles south of our farm and I'd heard was off the road that led to our church. The Rum was maybe 5 miles from our home. Well, I wanted to see it. It never occurred to me that I should tell anyone when I left to see the river, so I just took off. And I found it. It took a little exploration, but I found it. I can still see the gravel bar where I went down from the bank to walk along the river. And the freshwater clamshell that held a blister pearl. I knew that it was a pearl, but I wasn't picking things up that day, I was sightseeing. Then I went home. I was maybe a bit over half way there when my sister Carol found me. The whole family and neighborhood was out searching for me. I was mildly surprised – I'd not been lost, I knew where I was all along. And surely they knew that I had better sense than to get drowned or lost. So I had no idea why they were all upset.

The proper work of children, they say, is play (and school). I played pretty earnestly. Even I can remember making my perennial Christmas gift wish: a dump truck. And I had a succession of them, even though some of them cost nearly a dollar and we didn't have many dollars. Our yard was, like all farmyards then, dirt. I dug more dirt than I did in the Army or on my post-Army ditch digging job. I nearly undermined the "summer kitchen," a sort of shed near the house where we expanded our cooking when weather permitted. There was a pump in the middle of the yard where we got our water and where we stashed our butter in the cool well in the summer, and I dug around it until I bid fair to contaminate the water. I loved digging and pushing that dump truck around. I loved it so much that I got an itch - - scabies, tiny soil-dwelling mites that burrowed under my skin. Sulfur ointment and a vacation from digging cured that. Next summer, back to digging.

Other play was improvised. We didn't have much in the way of toys. I can remember coming home from the mailbox (a half mile away) with Carol when she got a mail-order doll with composition head, forearms, and legs. That was an event! I also vaguely remember breaking part of the doll some years later, I hope by accident such as stepping on it. With luck Carol will forgive me. We did have a checkers game board, and later Chinese checkers.

In the winter we were all closed up in that small house with its unheated attic and its walls insulated with old newspapers. Another memory is of playing beside the iron kitchen stove, making animals out of potatoes and matchsticks. (Yes, we were allowed to play with matches. Fire was a real thing, kindled in the iron kitchen stove and the round heating stove in the "living/dining" room. Kids knew about fire and we respected it. When we had a Christmas tree we clamped little candles on it, with a bucket of water standing by, and enjoyed the lights. And we lived through it.)

And we did have a library. Dad had made a bookcase while in Red Wing, solid quarter-sawn white oak, six feet tall and four feet wide, with a glass door over the bookshelves and with a drop-down desk on the right side. We had more books than almost anyone else in the surrounding two miles. People would borrow them, including our "doctor book," which we kids were not supposed to read. (One set of books was in Swedish: *History of Swedish Baptists in Minnesota.* Dad had written one of the chapters. We had some other Swedish books. Most of our neighbors spoke Swedish, and I didn't know anyone whose parents had been born in this country, and no one I knew over age 50 could speak intelligible English.)

We also had the only piano within 2 miles. Consequently our home was favored for neighborhood parties.

School is the other proper work of children. We kids went to school at an intersection called Elm Park, two miles due west of Stanchfield. That intersection is only that now -- the crossing of two country roads, with no buildings. But in those days there was a one-room school. When I started there, there were 30 kids in 8 grades and one teacher: Viola LaTourelle, fresh out of normal school, two years out of high school, on her first job. She was the best teacher I've ever had. In addition to doing her job well, she was lively and attractive. Brother Stan, only a couple of years younger than she, didn't get to first base.

I started school when I was just over five years old. There was no such thing as kindergarten of course, so I started in first grade. I remember my sister Ruth drilling me on the alphabet so that I could qualify. And I barely started school that year. On one of the first days I got into a mostly-verbal fight with the boy behind me. I claimed that he had taken my pencil. You can imagine that the teacher couldn't afford to have brawling among 30 kids aged 6 to 14, with no principal's office to send them to, and she tried to restore order by setting us in chairs in the front corners of the room, facing the wall. I stood for it for maybe a minute, then shook my fist at her and yelled, "Make me sit up here for nothing!" I was righteously indignant, as I vividly recall, because I was *right!* So I was expelled and my parents were advised to try next year.

Next year went pretty well. If I ever get around to the writing of "What Did You do in School, Daddy?" I'll tell more about that set of seminal experiences in the various halls of academe.

We went to church at Spring Vale Swedish Baptist five miles away. We walked to Sunday School and stayed (in the summer) for a picnic in the cemetery. That's a separate story in its own right which I'll write down some day if permitted. Hey, I'm old.

We grew potatoes. When the Depression frayed the social fabric, the price of potatoes became an issue on which everyone's livelihood depended. Then as now the small producer was at the mercy of the buyers. Dad joined the Great Potato Strike, an event that is probably not widely chronicled. I remember his going away at night. What he and other farmers did was to lay spiked boards across the roads to prevent truckers from hauling potatoes to the Cambridge potato warehouse. They were ready for bloodshed but I think that the strike ended up with some kind of compromise though with a lot of hard feelings.

To plant potatoes you used a hand-and-foot-operated potato planter. This was a pole with a hinged metal bill at the bottom, looking for all the world like a squared-off duck's bill. The rear of the bill was a continuation of the pole and a lever stuck out of the front of the forward part of the bill. This lever would open the bill at the right time.

First you cut your seed potatoes. You might buy them, or you might make do with potatoes left over from last year. There were only two kinds of potatoes then, russets and reds. You cut the potatoes into pieces that each had one or two eyes (these pieces are called seed potatoes), working in the evening before planting.

You put the cut potatoes into a bag made of gunnysack and slung it over your right shoulder and rested it on your left hip. In the field you lifted the planter with your right hand and reached into the sack with your left for a seed potato. You dropped the potato piece into the open top of the bill, thrust the bill into the ground, and pressed in down with your right foot. Then you rolled the top of the planter's pole forward and the lever on the front of the bill caused the bill to open and deposit the seed potato. Then you repeated, dragging your right foot over the hole to cover the seed. The rhythm was like a clodhopper ballet.

We raised corn, too. In those days there was no hybrid seed corn. You saved your own seed. There were two kinds of field corn, dent and flint. There were two kinds of sweet corn, Country Gentleman and Golden Bantam. We sent away to Gurney's for them because any sweet corn seed we'd saved would be crossed with field corn. There was also one kind of popcorn. We raised them all, on a small scale for hand planting and harvesting.

To plant corn you used a device made of two hinged boards, with the bottoms extended by a sheet metal bill and with round handles sticking sideways at the top. There was a metal seed reservoir on the side, with a slide that would pull out two or three kernels of corn and drop them into the bill when you closed it. You opened the handles, which closed the bill, and this dropped in the corn. Then you thrust the bill into the ground and opened the bill by bringing the top of the planter boards together. That deposited the seed in the ground. Then you dragged your foot over the hole to cover it and repeated the cycle. You got into a rhythm that moved you briskly down the row and spaced the hills of corn appropriately.

We had a garden. Like everybody else we raised any vegetables we intended to eat. The sandy soil was great for root vegetables like carrots, provided that you fertilized it. The horses and the cows took care of providing fertilizer. I was addicted to carrots, as were my brother Chester and especially my sister Carol. We stole carrots from the garden and stuck the tops back, thinking that we could fool Mom. We dug a secret cave in the sand bank beside the road and hid our loot there. I don't think that Mom was fooled, but I don't remember being punished.

We ate our corn, boiled if it was sweet corn, and loved it. We also ate field corn if we got it immature enough, and I don't remember it tasting any different from sweet corn. We made corn bread out of mature field corn, toasting the whole kernels in the oven and grinding them in the hand-cranked coffee grinder on the wall. You can get "corn meal" now, but it's degerminated and insipid. That was *real* corn meal.

Then there were the sheep. We tried raising a couple of them because in the Depression people tried everything. They grazed our yard. Then Mom sheared them, using a pair of those big spring-handled shears. She took the wool into Braham to have it washed and to have some of it spun into yarn (We didn't have a spinning wheel, although Mom had done her share of spinning in Norway.). When the wool came back we carded it into batts for filling quilts. Wool cards are rectangular boards with handles set across the wide dimension of the back, and with leather inner faces set with wire staples for teeth. I was pretty good at carding (so were the sibs, of course), and could make a decent batt and even make what Mom called in Norwegian a "tøl," a roll that could be fed through a spinning wheel. I helped Mom to hank-dye some of the yarn, dipping half of the hank into blue dye. From that yarn Mom first made me a sweater that I wore for years until it came apart. Then Mom unraveled it and knitted mittens for me. When they failed, she unraveled it again and knitted mittens for Daughter Eileen. Those mittens are now mounted on Daughter Katy's wall.

The sheep produced more than wool. They produced high-quality fertilizer. As you recall, we were in the depths of Hard Times, with everyone so poor that no one was aware of being poor. Mom took over a half acre of sandy hillock (In that flat country, a rise of two feet made a hillock) next to the road and dug in sheep manure. Then she sent away for strawberry plants, both June bearers and Mastodon Everbearing. She planted and nursed them through a first, poorly-productive summer, carrying water in a pail (I hope we kids helped her). The second year, they bore. And we were the only source of strawberries in the county. We picked berries and sold them to the general store in Stanchfield and to neighbors and passers-by at ten cents a quart.

We became the neighborhood capitalists. We hired neighbors to pick strawberries at a penny a quart. Those were great times. The strawberries were our cash crop at a time of the year before other crops were ripe. Strawberries are still my favorite fruit. I couldn't have been as good at picking as the others, but a fond memory is of going back to the house with permission to eat a half-quart with sugar and cream. One such session was with the quart box that was filled by just seven berries.

My Aunt Gina near Isanti also raised strawberries. By the time other people caught onto the economics of raising strawberries the Depression was starting to break and we were moving on to another farm.

By then I was ten years old and a regular farm worker. I milked cows (as did my sibs). Our farm, of course, had neither phone nor electricity, so we milked by hand. We didn't get carpal tunnel syndrome but the muscles and tendons on the inside of the forearm ached like crazy after 3 or 4 cows. We took the warm milk into the house and ran it through the hand-cranked cream separator. The cream went to town, Stanchfield, to the creamery.

Once in a while I got to go along. It was great to watch the cream being tested in the Babcock machine: cream and acid into a test tube, then a whirl in a small centrifuge to determine the butterfat content and consequently the price. We kids could drink all the cold buttermilk we wanted at the creamery, just about the only cold drink available in the summer. (Stanchfield had electricity, but no farms did. So, no refrigeration.) Stores sell "buttermilk" now, but it's really soured skim milk. That buttermilk was tangy with tiny bits of butter floating in it. And the butter was made from sour cream because farmers didn't have refrigeration. That was butter with natural flavor. Now butter is made from sweet cream, then yellow color is added along with lactic acid from sour milk, without which it would taste like lard.

We made our own butter at times, too. We had a stoneware churn with a wooden dasher that fitted through a hole in the lid. Later we had a butter churn that consisted of a square gallon glass jar topped by a cast iron gearbox with a crank. You turned the crank and wooden paddles in the jar stirred the cream into butter.

In the other childhood story, the one I'll write later if permitted, I'll tell you about the use of lard on bread when you can't afford to keep any of your cream.

The Great Depression was the first of the three great shaping experiences of the Twentieth Century (the other two being World Wars I & II, and the Viet Nam War). It's hard to define the lessons we learned from it, though some can be pointed out as obvious.

We learned that we could survive. We took the worst that the economy could throw at us and we survived. We maybe didn't live the high life but we lived and, in non-material ways, we lived well. We laughed just as much as people do now; probably more. We had sturdier family relationships than now even though we may have had to swallow more interpersonal stress without passing it off as the fault of society or of poor self-image. We had real parties with friends who were as mixed as our neighborhood (in our case, that wasn't very mixed, though we did have a couple of Norwegians, a Welshman, and a Lebanese man who didn't go to parties). We had time out of a day that was regular as clockwork (everyone had chores with livestock, but that ended about 6 PM). We had evenings together with the family, partly because there was no place to go (by modern standards). We read a lot, even though the wick-fired kerosene lamp was dim. What a great event when we got an Aladdin mantle lamp!

We learned what it was to be poor, in the sense of being without money. Elegance was going to school with a handkerchief that was a square cut out of a flour sack, but *hemmed*! We never learned that there could be such a thing as a culture of poverty because we didn't feel impoverished. Sure, there were a couple of families who lived the dysfunctional life we now associate with poverty, but they didn't lack money any more than the rest of us. Though they did lack some common sense in managing their limited resources. When people now say, "Money isn't everything," we know the truth of the cliché.

We sang. We didn't listen to someone else make music, we sang. Everybody did, whether or not they sang well. Some of the Depression era songs we sang were designed to pick up our spirits, and to younger people they now sound corny and naive when we trot them out. But in the 1930s they were genuine. We sang hymns. If anyone is interested in what we sang, he need only pick up a copy of *The Golden Book of Favorite Songs*. This was our public school songbook. A substantial section was hymns and real Christmas songs. No one called in the Civil Liberties Union on us. Some of the songs are offensive now, now that there are people who have, for political reasons, made occasions for offense when none was intended nor taken at the time (wait 50 years; some modern songs and themes will be anathema to your children). But the point is that we sang and it helped us to keep our spirits up.

We had faith. Not just the faith of religion, though we had that and were neither ashamed of it nor ridiculed for it. We also had the faith of people who knew, from personal experience or the experience of their parents, what the alternatives to America were. And yes, in a decade we learned that our faith was more justified than we knew at the time. We were innocent of the pervasive cynicism that later became the hallmark of the cultured citizen. We knew that, if we could get through the next few years, we would come out on top.

All that came with the territory. It was part of being a farmer. Even more than today, being a farmer was more than an occupation. It was a way of life. And everyone in the family, not just the father, was a farmer. That came with the territory, too. So all those things about total life that I mention above were part of being a farmer, the first thing I did for a living.

THE SECOND FARM
Diamond Bluff, Wisconsin, 1934 to 1942

As I said earlier, we moved when I was ten years old. We moved to a 160-acre farm in Wisconsin near Diamond Bluff and ten miles away from Red Wing across the Mississippi. This was some farm. It was all yellow clay, and the buildings were down in a valley with some of the fields on the flatland and some on top of each of the flanking bluffs, maybe 300 feet higher. Half of the farm, as we used to say, was straight up and the other half was straight down. There was a public road that led up the western bluff to our fields up there, and a farm road barely passable by wagon leading up to our eastern fields on the other bluff.

Now we expanded our operations. We had the biggest house in the neighborhood, with 11 rooms. When it had been built it was the showplace of the area and it had had gas lighting then. We did almost as well. A few years earlier we had graduated from flat-wick kerosene lamps to Aladdin mantle lamps. The white light was almost blinding -- you could read by it even if you were six feet away.

And we had running water! Half way up the hill behind the house was a windmill with a big underground reservoir. So water was piped into the house, but of course there was no sewer or septic tank. We used the outhouse, and water from the sink dropped down to a bucket which we then took out and emptied. There apparently had been a drain, no longer connected, with which the original owner had piped drain water out to the side and spread onto the ground above the barnyard. All that was left was a broken end of clay drainpipe in the side yard.

In our later years on the farm, we got a gasoline-powered washing machine. Its muffler was no great shakes. I can still hear its putt-putt as it sounded at the end of our farm, down to the south border. But it represented progress.

A few years ago I found a contour map of Wisconsin that showed our valley. It has a name: Hope Coulee. We knew it as a water hazard when we had a heavy rain, and especially in Spring run-off. Then the water would roar down between our house/barn/granary compound and our mailbox beside the road on the other side, with the water sometimes five feet deep. It would spread out across the flats, leaving shawls of weed wrapped across the bottoms of the fence posts. Once the run-off was so heavy that it dragged an all-steel peg-tooth harrow a couple of hundred feet into the pasture. Between rains the gully was dry, a rutted path through yellow clay. Farther downstream, in the Steen's pasture, the gully had cut into the clay in a square bottomed canyon, fifty to 100 feet wide and 25 feet deep. The Steen boys and I used it as a Wild West playground, trying to hit each other with spears made of giant ragweed stems. Now the gully has moved upstream, and it has completely cut the old driveway. The road to the farm buildings now comes in through what was the cornfield.

On the hills, and especially in the rocky gullies that cut deep Vs in the bluffs, there were fossils. Most were, by my present standards, pretty poor and blurry, but that's where I got started in fossil collecting. Of all the neighbors only the Steen boys shared my enthusiasm. The rest thought that we were crazy to look for rocks. I have uncharitable opinions about the vision of our neighbors.

But in this essay, I want to talk mostly about work. Everyone who lives on a farm is a worker, and I was then a mature ten.

There were more cows to milk. We sometimes had a dozen going at once. I dealt with both ends of the cows, too. They were stalled below the huge hayloft. My job was to pitch hay down the chute and then serve it up in the mangers. When they were done with the hay I cleaned the barn. A gutter in the floor held their products, and a cable-mounted trolley bucket was brought indoors to receive the load. Then the trolley was run out into the barnyard and tripped, depositing the fragrant load onto the manure pile.

The four horses were stalled in the barn, too. Their product had its own unique smell. When you cleaned their stalls you had to frequently go outside, teary and gasping from the ammonia.

We had two new horses in Wisconsin. They were Percherons, Knute and Prince. Knute was just about six feet tall at the shoulders, with feet the size of washtubs. He had a sense of humor. When you went into his stall to harness him, he stood quietly enough. But when you were occupied with getting the harness over his high back, he would slyly reach over with his right forefoot and trap your foot under it - not enough to hurt, but enough so that you couldn't get out. Then he'd lean, ever so slowly, to the right and press you against the side of the stall. When you yelled, "Knute!" and whacked him with your hand, he'd look surprised and take the foot off you. Sixteen hundred pounds of humor.

But those horses were a wonder. We had to take wagon loads of hay or grain down from those blufftop fields, and everybody else had to chain-lock a rear wheel of their wagons to go down such steep hills. Not us. Knute would place his rump against the front of the wagon, brace his oversize feet, and let Prince steer the wagon down the hill, with Knute skidding most of the way.

I spent many hours looking at the rumps of those horses, and the rumps of the other two, Tom and Daisy.

We used the smaller horses for tasks like cultivating corn.

A horse-drawn cultivator is a two-wheeled implement with a set of three-inch-wide shovels that gouged down the furrows between the corn to root out weeds. (We didn't have herbicides or any pesticides except Paris green.) Because there would be rocks in the fields, the shovels had to be able to break away instead of breaking off. That was accomplished by wooden pegs that held the hinged shovels in place until a stone sheared off the pegs. So I would drive the horses down the field for a couple of long rows, then rest them while I found and whittled sticks into pegs to replace those that sheared off.

(One of a farmer's best friends in those days was a jackknife. It had to be kept sharp, and a lost knife was a catastrophe. Other hand tools were necessary, too. When you were ten miles from town, a half hour's drive in a car burning gas that cost 19 cents a gallon, you had to be resourceful. Break a pitman rod on the mower? make a new one from a piece of lumber, oak if you had it. If you broke one of your tools there was usually no avoiding the trip to town. I remember going with Dad to Red Wing to have a broken wood plane brazed. Son Don has that plane now, I think, along with Dad's tool box. Dad was great with wood, having been a carpenter, and he made good use of the plane and the drawknife and the hand saw - we had only one saw, of course, and he sharpened it himself. Farmers had to be resourceful.)

Wood was part of our livelihood, too. We got all our winter heat from wood, as well as all our cooking fuel. Our new farm had about half of its area in pasture, much of it wooded. Wood, as they say, warms you twice: once when you cut it, and once when you burn it. We cut all our own wood. Red oak was the best. To cut a tree, you notch it with an axe to determine its direction of fall, then two of you get on the "misery whip," the six-foot, two-man crosscut saw. You bend over the handle, and fall into a reciprocal rhythm, each of you pulling in turn. Eventually the tree crashes down right where you planned, and you swamp off the branches. The trunk and the big branches are skidded out of the woods by the horses, with you dancing along beside the log and trying not to get pinned against a stump.

We often hired a saw rig to cut the wood into stove lengths. For much of the wood we cut the logs with a bucksaw, but for really serious work you hired a sawyer. He came and set up a three-foot, unguarded circular saw on a stand, belted it to his tractor, and you fed logs across it. The big saw rang and sang as it whizzed through the logs, and the chunks piled up. All of us stacked it for winter.

Splitting chunks was by hand, of course. Most people used a single-bit axe, but I preferred the balance and straight handle of the double-bit. When the temperature was about zero you set a red oak chunk upright on the chopping block and swung. The axe would hardly sink in before the oak would crack and spring apart. Oh, oak is great stuff to split. But cottonwood: I remember trying to split a green chunk of that. The axe would sink in, grunt, and stop. You'd wrench it out and try again. One day, I broke an axe handle by striking too hard with too much follow-through.

We didn't raise much potato on our new farm. The soil was too heavy for good root growth. But we did raise corn and grain.

We cut the corn by hand for the first few of our eight years there. You tucked the cornstalks of a hill under your left arm, and swung a corn knife to cut off all the stalks. Most people used a sort of serrated sickle, but I favored a corn knife that resembled a square-nosed machete. In fact, I used that knife for dozens of things around the farm. Once I repaired a break in the fence by stripping down some elm bark with the knife and tying the fence together. As far as I know, it's still holding.

Anyhow, you then stacked the corn from several hills into a corn shock, a pyramid maybe three feet across the base and seven feet high. You bound it with binder twine. Later you took a wagon into the field and pitched the bundles onto it for the trip to the barn. There you shucked as much as you needed to by hand, and later fed stalks and ears to the cows. The shucked corn was for the chickens and the pigs. We didn't have a silo to store ensilage. (You look it up; I'm not going to spell out everything.)

Later, we got a horse-drawn, two-row mechanical corn picker, but I don't remember doing much of that. Maybe, as the youngest, I was considered unfit for such dangerous work. People lost arms and legs in those things. I didn't drive the manure spreader often, either, probably for the same reason. The whirling blades at the rear of the spreader couldn't distinguish between manure and people.

I did do a lot of hay mowing and raking. The mower was drawn by two horses and a foot lever dropped the sickle bar down at the right side. Then a pitman rod rammed the triangular knives on the sickle back and forth to cut the hay. I guess that the mower was dangerous, too, but none of us worried. We knew that its mission in life was to cut, and we took care with it. But we lost our dog to it. A hired man was mowing and wasn't careful nor did he mention what had happened. When we searched for the dog, Stan found it still alive. He carried Bud home, covered his eyes, and put him out of his misery. You have to be able to do that.

The dump-rake was also a two-wheeled implement, horse-drawn of course, but its wheels were 'way out on the ends of it. It was a dozen feet wide, and I sat on an iron seat above the axle. The rake teeth were semi-circles with springs coiled in their inboard ends. A long hand lever allowed me to retract the teeth when we were trundling to the field, then I dropped the teeth down to drag the cut hay. When a respectable rakeful was dragged up, then I'd stamp on the foot lever and a sprag would engage the hub of one wheel and the teeth would pull up and deposit the hay. Going around the field, I'd make long windrows of hay, ready to be pitched up onto the hayrack.

Loading the hayrack was another of my joys. It always happened in the hottest part of summer, humid with the threat of rain that impelled us to hurry and get the hay in. A three-tined pitchfork was the standard tool. One of us would be up on the wagon, driving the horses and arranging the hay so that it would be picked up by the hayfork.

Our barn had a big sliding door through which the wagon could be backed between the two haylofts. Then we unhitched the horses and hitched them to the hayrope.

This long, thick rope was threaded through pulleys and ended up on a track that ran the length of the barn up at the peak. A set of catches on the track set the limits for the trolley that carried the hayfork. This fork was a two-pronged affair, wickedly sharp-looking as it came down to the person who was setting it in the hayload. One of us (usually me) took the fork, two and a half feet across, and jammed it two feet down into the hay load. Then I'd pull up the levers that set the toggles, making it into a double harpoon that would pick up the hay. I'd yell that it was ready, then the horses would be driven away from the barn. A cubic yard of hay would rise up to the track overhead, click off the stop, and roll to a spot over the hay mow. I'd yell again, and jerk the trip-rope that would release the harpoon toggles and thereby the hay, which would drop with a "whoosh!" and a gust of dust. Then I'd pull back the hayfork by its trip-rope and we'd repeat till the wagon was empty. It sure beat pitching the hay into the mow by hand.

Another crop that involved pitching and wagons was the grain. We raised oats, some wheat, and barley. The seed was put into the ground with a two-horse grain drill. This was a two-wheeled implement with a long seed box set over the eight-foot axle. Gears from the wheels drove the mechanism that pulled a few grains every few inches and dropped them down into funnels that led to angled disks that cut into the ground and buried the seed, in rows five inches or so apart. A chain dragged on the ground behind each set of disks, covering the seed. Grain, because it grew so thick, could not be cultivated. We did pull some weeds by hand, mostly Canadian thistles. Dad could pull them with his bare hands, but we kids weren't callused enough. Grain mostly took care of itself if we'd prepared the ground properly.

Then came harvest. We cut grain with a binder, a sort of mower with accessories. Over the sickle bar rotated a big wooden reel, which rotated backwards, with horizontal bars that bent the grain over the sickle bar and dropped it into the apron. This apron was a canvas belt that conveyed the grain, neatly laid side-by-side and with the heads to the rear, into a bundler where the stalks were gathered together. Then an ingenious hooked lever would reach across with sisal twine pulled off a big spool, and tie the bundle and drop it behind the binder. A line of tied bundles of grain would stitch across the field.

Dad usually drove the binder, though we all had our turns. We would follow behind and pick up the bundles two at a time. We set the first pair upright, braced against each other, gathered other pairs and leaned them together, and capped the shock with a bundle laid sideways to shed any rain. The result was a field studded with shocks that would shed rain.

Then came threshing. On our first farm, we would stack the bundles into a cone maybe 20 feet high beside the barn, built with the heads inward around a pole. Then a steam powered thresher would tour the neighborhood, to thresh grain well into fall. This was called "stack threshing."

On our second farm, we were in a different social and acreage situation. There we neighbors banded together to bring in and thresh the grain together. We called this "field threshing."

Half a dozen or more farms would make up a threshing crew. We would contract for a threshing rig to make the rounds of the farms. All the neighbors, following a complicated formula of workers and teams, would work together. We went to their farms; they came to ours.

When our turn came the threshing rig would pull into the farmyard and set up. We were modern. The power was a gasoline tractor, driving the dinosaur-like thresher with a long belt from the tractor's power takeoff pulley. The operator would line things up and try it out the evening before, usually.

Then we would all go to the grain fields. Our farm provided one wagon and massive team, and usually three hands: Dad, Brother Chester, and me. The wagons would go down each row of grain shocks, and one or two men would walk along and pitch those bundles onto the load. There might be two men on the wagon, one to drive and one to stack. The work was hot and itchy, especially if there was barley, with its scroll-saw beards. And it was hard work, too. My peak was pitching 13 loads of rye, a grain with long and heavy stems, in one day.

When the wagon was loaded it was driven to the farmyard and parked beside the thresher. One or two men would pitch bundles from the load onto the intake chute of the thresher. Inside the machine, bars and knives would beat the bundles into bits, and blow the chaff off the grain and out a long pipe onto a straw pile. The grain would cascade from a side chute into bags or into a wagon box, to be stored for sale or for farm use.

Noon-time, and we came in to eat. You've heard the expression, "eating like a threshing crew." There was a lot of truth behind that expression. The homemaker, with any daughters available and sometimes with the help of a neighbor woman, would prepare enough food to choke a whale. And it never was too much. Roast or meatballs or pork chops, lots of potatoes and gravy, pitchers of coffee and lemonade, and at least two kinds of pie, were obligatory. Woe to the homemaker who underestimated the appetites of the threshing crew! Her stinginess would be the talk of the neighborhood for years.

The other work of a child, play and school, continued. My new school was smaller, with only 16 of us in the eight grades in one room. Again, it was two miles away, but this time up and over the bluff.

It wasn't a friendly place for a shy, bookwormish, frail kid. Fights in the schoolyard were common. A classmate, Mike, took great delight in pummeling me every chance he got. (Forty years later, I met him again and asked him why he did it. Turns out that he just enjoyed it: "I dunno, I just liked to do it.") Matters improved after I found out that I could run faster than Mike, and after I tried a trick I'd read about. Mike always came in with his head down, chopping upward with both fists. I grabbed him by the ears and cracked his nose across my knee. But Mike was not alone. Once I was the target of a half dozen stompers, who broke two of my ribs. I found out the damage years later, when I had a chest X-ray. At the time, my chest hurt, but what's the big deal for a farm boy?

Let's mention another feature of rural school that may seem strange in an urban setting, and I suppose would seem strange in even a rural school now, 70 years later. That's the boy's knife. We all carried knives to school. How else could we play mumbly-peg? You opened the spear blade (the long one) all the way, and the pen blade (the shorter one, on the same hinge) half way. Then you flipped the knife to make it stick in the ground. First, you stuck the spear blade into the ground and flipped the knife into the air with a finger under the end of the handle; if the pen blade didn't stick enough to support the knife, or if the spear blade didn't stick upright enough in the ground to allow you to slip at least one finger under the end of the handle, you lost that turn and the other guy made his move. If he succeeded, then he went on to the next move, which was to put the tip of the spear blade on his knee and flip the knife forward; again, success was to get the spear blade to stick in the ground. This went on inventively: flip off the toe of the shoe, flip off an elbow, flip off a shoulder. Whoever succeeded in most moves, won.

Carrying a knife was not dangerous. Every kid from age five knew how to handle a knife and treated a knife as sharp. The kid learned about edges the first time he closed his knife without getting his finger out of the way. We had serious fights on the schoolground, but no one ever pulled a knife. If he had, everyone would have turned on him, he'd have been sent home, his parents would have taken the hide off him, and that would be the end of it. Or so we thought, though no one ever tested it. We respected knives. Come to think of it, if I were faced with a fight and had to fight for my life then or now, I'd skip the jack-knife and pick up a softball bat. It's much more effective, but modern schools don't ban bats. Go figure.

For more of my grade school career, see the book I hope to write on "What Did You Do in School, Daddy?"

After four years in the Wisconsin grade school, I went on to high school in Red Wing. But let's save that for the "What Did You Do in School, Daddy?" book.

Play as such became less frequent for an older boy on a busy farm, but I found ways. From digging in the dirt, I turned to scouting for fossils. That part of Wisconsin is famous for its Ordovician fossils, and I found more of them than anyone. Thus began a lifelong hobby.

Chester and I went fishing when we could, too. We'd walk the two or three miles to the Mississippi, after we outgrew fishing for chubs in the little Trimbel Creek, and went after carp and bullheads. I had somehow fallen heir to a bamboo fly rod, and with that I caught carp up to five pounds. I tried casting for bigger fish, too, but that ended when I practice-cast with Stan's jointed hollow-steel casting rod - with no line - and the end section sailed out into the river and was lost forever. But with the fly rod and cane poles we caught significant fish. One afternoon we caught 42 bullheads, and brought most of them home. Bullheads are tough; after a two-mile walk home, some of them were still alive. We caught a rare northern pike, and some buffalo fish. Our family was still not out of its financial depression, and fish was meat.

I bought a little .22 rifle from Cousin Almon for a whole dollar, and shot squirrels for stew. We had snared rabbits on both farms. Meat was meat. For more substantial meat, we usually butchered pigs. Only once or twice did we kill a calf. Veal sold for too good a price for us to eat the things.

We raised pigs. As I grew, I took more part in the bloody part of pig raising. We caused sterility in male pigs when they were fairly young. For this task every farmer's jackknife had a spay blade. We'd flip the pig onto its back and operate. My job was usually to hold the back feet against the belly. As soon as we were done, the pig would right itself, cease screaming, and root about for food. Sometimes I wielded the knife.

We butchered pigs, usually in the late fall when the weather was cool enough to help preserve the meat. We'd lead the pig to the site beside a pulley in the drive-through center of the corn crib, next to a barrel of boiling water. One of us (usually Stan) would stun the pig with the blunt side of an axe, and expertly stick it to bleed. Then we'd hoist the pig on the pulley and dip it in the hot water to loosen the hair. Out of the water the pig was laid on a board table and shaved. Not exactly shaved, because instead of cutting of the hairs, we'd scrape them out by the roots, which was the rationale for the hot water. Sometimes we'd use a plain butcher knife to do the shaving, sometimes sharp-edged bell-shaped disks on a short handle. Once shaved and rinsed, the pig would be hoisted again and gutted. Then we'd saw it in half for further butchering. (You don't like the gore? Sorry, but a farmer knows how meat gets to the table, because he got it there; he knows that it doesn't come into existence in a plastic package.)

Mom was the expert on cutting up and preserving the meat. I'd help, and learned a lot of anatomy that way. The head was cleaned up and made into - what else? - head cheese. The fat was set aside to be rendered into lard. The bigger cuts of meat were salted down with Morton's Smoke Salt in the 30-gallon stoneware crock.

We ground the fat in the meat grinder to make it ready for rendering. Pans of the fat would be set in the oven and the over-sweet aroma of rendering would fill the house. Mom always made special lard from the pig's omentum, the veil of fatty tissue that covers the intestines, because is was the most delicate. That was for special cooking, like cookies. We could eat the crackling, the defatted tissue that remained from rendering, as snacks. Or we could find it in "klub," the patties of grated potatoes that are boiled and were served with butter.

Altogether, in those dim days of the 1930s, we lived a fairly self-sufficient life on the farm.

But it was work. Don't kid yourself; a farm boy works, from the time he's old enough to be useful. We usually didn't think of it as work, we though of it as living. But it laid the foundation of all the later things I did for a living.

Even work can be made interesting. We usually had cats in the barn with us when we milked the cows, and cats, of course, like milk. It began as the sport of occasionally hitting the cat with a squirt of milk. A cow makes a good squirt gun. The cat would lick off the milk, and eventually learn to come back for more. From that we moved on to hitting the cat in the face, and the cat learned to open its mouth. I'd move the squirt higher, and the cat would sit up straight. Then I'm move the stream of milk away, and the cat would bat at it with its paw. From then on, I'd say, "Heil Milksquirt!" and the cat would sit up straight and stretch out a paw in a credible Nazi salute. I had most of our cats trained (although, come to think of it, I didn't know anything about operant conditioning or successive approximation then, and the cats were probably training me.)

Then, seemingly all at the same time, we were in World War II and life changed. We moved to Red Wing, I graduated from high school and went to Bethel Junior College for a semester, and then I entered the Army. For that, you'll have to read *What Did You Do in the War, Daddy?*

SEWER PIPE, POTTERY, AND NURSERY WORKER
EARLY 1940s

It was a long time ago, and I was a feckless youth. So I may have my chronology a bit mixed up, but the essentials are correct.

It was, I think, right after graduation from high school, and I needed a job. There was a brief stint as a worker in the local factory that made buna rubber, the first of the synthetic rubbers that was later supplanted by butyl rubber.

Then I signed on as a worker in the local sewer pipe factory. It was there that I was issued my Social Security card. My job was to bear off ware from the extruder.

To make sewer pipe, the clay was extruded from a machine that molded three-foot lengths of pipe, in my case about eight inches inside diameter. The machine would deposit the completed section of pipe on a platform under the extruding nozzle and lift up to start the next section. My job was to pick up the green section (stiff, though still moist clay) and set it on a pallet beside the machine. This entailed taking about 30 pounds of clay in front of me, turning to the left, and setting down the load at a lower level. All this, as any modern safety engineer would immediately perceive, is exactly designed to rupture a spinal disk. It did. I went home the third day with a mighty sore back and spent several days in bed. That ended that career.

In those days we not only didn't have OSHA, we didn't have worker's compensation either. So I got my termination paycheck and that was that. I recovered, and a year later I was accepted by the Army. And a few years after that, I spent three years in a back brace. All my subsequent life I've had backaches and occasional episodes of disablement, but now the disk is so old and dried out that it can't do any more harm.

Soon after, I took a job in the Red Wing Potteries. I told the personnel man that I wasn't going to college, and he accepted the statement even though we both knew it to be fiction. My title was fettler. My job was to take the green ware (that's pottery that may have been dried but not fired) from the man who was glazing it and swipe off the drying glaze from the parts that were going to touch the kiln car.

A fettler uses a two-inch square of steel, grinding it to suit the contours of the ware he's working on. Usually, I worked on cookie jars and their lids. The glazer would position the jar over a jet of water-based glaze to glaze the inside, drain it, and then set it upright on a turntable and spray more glaze on the outside of the jar. I'd take it, and scrape the glaze from the bottom, the part that would sit on the kiln car. Then I'd scrape the glaze from the part of the rim that would receive the lid, as well as from the rim of the lid, so that the two parts could be fired in matched sets but not be welded together by melted glaze.

I'd stack the jars on the kiln car. This was an iron cart with sand-sprinkled firebrick surfaces, running on small-scale railroad tracks. The jars would be stacked so as to not touch each other, and when the car was full it would be trundled to the kiln to be dragged slowly through the firing. In the tunnel of the kiln, gas jets would raise the temperature to 1800 degrees. You could look through small ports on the kiln and see the ware glowing red-hot on the cars. Then came a cooling section, and the ware would emerge 24 hours after entry, cool enough to handle and with the finished glaze hardened into glass.

My two sisters, Ruth and Carol, also worked at the potteries, but they were skilled workers. They did hand-painting of under-glaze designs. Their workroom was not far from my station, but it was a story higher. I recall that I did get up to see that shop, but I don't recall anything about it.

I got to see other parts of the potteries, too. One operation that fascinated me was the making of flower pots. In this, the worker took a ball of clay and plopped it into the lower mold cavity. He pressed two switches and a spinning upper mold, with a spike for the hole in the bottom of the flower pot, would drop down and press the clay, and withdraw upward, still spinning. The bottom of the mold would pop up, and the worker would take off the finished pot and plop in another ball of clay. Come to think of it now, I don't think that there were switches. I think that the worker had to time his motions so as not to get caught by a lowering upper mold. Safety devices were new in those days.

The most skilled molding job at the potteries was that of making the large stoneware crocks, five to 30 gallons. In this operation there was only the spinning bottom mold, with its cavity in the shape of the crock's outer surface. The worker would drop in a ball of clay, and then reach down into the spinning mold with a rectangular wooden fid, and draw the clay up the sides and over the rim. He had to know exactly how to draw the clay to uniform thickness, because there were no guides. If he pressed down on the bottom too hard, the clay would get too thin. Similarly, if he didn't get the sides vertical, the top or the bottom of the sidewall would be too thick or too thin. He had to get all of it just under an inch thick for the larger crocks, maybe thinner for the smaller ones. These workers never talked while they worked.

I worked that job for some months before resigning to go to college. As a part-time job while a student at Bethel Junior College in St. Paul, I took employment with the Rose Nursery on Larpenter Avenue. There, I mostly cut dahlia roots into plantable sections before storage. The work was out in the fields. I still have a small scar on each thigh where the back end of the pruning shears snapped shut after a tough cut. The job was fairly short, less than a month as I recall.

Next spring, after I'd quite Bethel and moved back to Red Wing to await my Army call, expected in April but postponed until July, I took a job as a laborer with the Red Wing Nursery. This was educational and I've used the training I got there all my life in amateur horticulture.

I did everything they do in nurseries. I balled evergreens, for example. There, you use a sharp nursery spade to cut the tree loose from the soil without breaking the ball of soil around the roots, then you wrap the soil ball in burlap before cutting the pedestal loose. There is, of course, some trick to it, and the largest tree I was able to ball by myself weighed maybe 300 pounds.

The nursery spade became a familiar tool. One day out on planting job, we had to dig and cut up an eight-inch elm and we had forgotten to bring an axe. I cut down, and cut up, that tree with the spade. Ever since, as my kids can verify, I've had a fetish about keeping a sharp nursery spade.

Our crew landscaped one of the big historical houses in Hastings. Even now when I drive by the grounds I can see our design still visible.

The nursery stocked irises, and when they bloomed I was able to not only take home blossoms for the table, but I kept track of which ones we wanted to plant at home. I'm still an iris fan.

The nursery job ended, as I recall, when I was drafted into the Army. Read *What Did You Do in the War, Daddy?* to find out all about that. Here, only an outline.

ARMY LIFE
1943 to 1946

Another publication, *What Did You Do in the War, Daddy?* gives all the details of that experience.

Briefly: I entered military service in July, 1943 from Fort Snelling, and became a Light Ponton Engineer. Our company, the 537th Engineer LP Co., specialized in building floating bridges and Bailey (tinker-toy) bridges, and in furnishing assault boats and foot bridges for river crossings. I was officially a Rigger, but I rode shotgun with my .50 caliber machine gun on the air compressor and ration trucks.

I served in France, landing 59 days after D-Day, and in Luxemburgh and Germany. The ETO ribbon for our unit carries four battle stars (Normandy, France, Ardennes, Germany). I ended the war in the extreme southeast corner of Germany, then was sent to Marseilles, and was demobilized in January, 1946.

In many ways, World War II shaped the lives of us who took part in it. For me, it came after the first semester of college, and the GI Bill and the education it enabled opened up to me my options so that I became a professional worker rather than a laborer or a craftsman. Maybe I'd have made more money as a craftsman, but in my professional career I lived more of the life that I wanted.

When I returned from the Army in 1946 I went back to school. During that summer, as a traditional summer job, I dug ditches -- literally. The sewer system of Red Wing was being expanded west of Twin Bluffs and a crew of us young bucks did the pick and shovel work. Great exercise.

PATHOLOGY ATTENDANT
1946 to 1948

Life as a college student resumed in January of 1946. Since I'd been discharged on January 6, there was no time to be wasted in reporting back to Bethel Junior College for the resumption of what had been a one-semester Freshman year. But now Bethel had gone onto the quarter system, so I re-entered in the middle of the Winter quarter. No harm. For example, C. E. Carlson's class picked up exactly where it had been in 1943, according to my notes. Well, not exactly - there was a 20-minute overlap, in which he repeated a joke that I'd noted down three years earlier.

(For the rest of student affairs, see the separate "*What Did You do in School, Daddy?*"- assuming that it gets written.)

After the first few weeks, after I had done some planning and had had some free GI counseling, medical school became my goal. Actually, when I saw the counselor and reviewed my test grades, the counselor hit the roof. "What do you mean, getting Bs and Cs? From now on, you pull straight As!" That was before the era of non-directive counseling, and vocational counselors were supposed to know more about your potential, after testing it, than you did.

Anyhow, that meant that I'd have used up all my GI Bill eligibility before I got to that expensive medical school. So I asked that the government terminate my support, and save it for later. That was all right with them.

Consequently I looked for part-time work in the fall of 1946. Living at Bethel, then just across the street from the State Fair Grounds, it was natural to look to the kinds of work other students were doing. There was a bunch of students working part time at Wards, just down Snelling Avenue at University Avenue, but that didn't seem to be my style. But there was another smaller bunch who worked at old Ancker Hospital on West Seventh Street in St. Paul (now Regions Hospital in a different location), mostly on night or swing shifts. That did appeal, especially in view of my goal in medicine.

Paul Wage was my mentor in this. Paul, a short and dark fellow student who was credible in his claim to be Indian, had worked at Ancker before. So he and I went down there to be interviewed. Paul took the lead, and he went back to talk to the interviewer after we had finished. Then he came out, and we found out what our jobs would be. Paul, bless his generous heart, had taken the opening as orderly on the swing shift, and left to me the job of pathology attendant. I will never forget his generosity.

My hours would be from 6 to 10 five nights a week, with a room in the Men's Service Building at the hospital. One meal a day was included, the big late-evening meal. This gave me free room and half board. And the room came with weekly maid cleanup and linen changes.

Best yet, I was on call, not on active duty. If I was needed in the lab, I went. Otherwise I was free to study in the room or go and volunteer at any place in the hospital I found interesting. No lab work was scheduled after 10 PM, except for Coroner's emergencies. And I could be roused at any time up to 6 AM to release bodies to undertakers.

For this, they also paid me. My wage was $70 per month, a substantial sum in those days. I paid my tuition, books, and other living expenses. And I always, and for the first time in civilian life, walked around with money in my pocket.

The job of lab attendant at Ancker was an education in itself. My job was to assist at autopsies.

They gave me a tour of orientation, and I reported for work. When I got to my room the first night, the phone rang. I was wanted in the lab.

To the lab I went, and there the staff pathologist and the resident pathologist were just completing an autopsy - a "post." I will never know whether this was a test of my ability to handle the job, because the body was open and the organs were in trays, and the pathologist said, "Put it together," and left. It's a good thing that I was a farm boy, familiar with the realities of anatomy. A person and a hog look and smell the same internally.

The resident stayed long enough to tell me how to go about the task. You put the organs back in the body cavity (sorry about the way this sounds, but I'll spare you some of the graphics) and sew up the incision. You use a sacking needle and cotton store twine, with a baseball stitch. Then you shift the body onto a gurney cart, drape it, and take it to the next room, the columbarium, where there are refrigerated trays onto which you move the body. Unless it's a very large person, this is a one-man job. You roll the tray back into the cabinet, and everything is ready for the undertaker.

Normally, and on the average of two nights a week for two years, I assisted at the autopsy itself. The phone would ring and I'd report to the lab. The pathologist and the resident would get there about the same time and we'd gown and mask and pull on rubber gloves. Sometimes we'd get there before the body, and the delivering orderly would help to move it onto the slab. Sometimes the body would be already in the columbarium.

The slab was a white porcelain table on a pedestal in the middle of the room. At the "foot" end of the room was a small gallery where student nurses would very occasionally be brought to witness their obligatory autopsy.

After 48 years, I bet I could still carry out the routine of assistance, if the Noble routine was followed.   John Noble was the head pathologist who ruled the lab with absolute confidence. You do a post one way - his way.

(Note: many people just don't want to know how a post is done, even if it's the right way. So, in deference to the squeamish, I've made an optional appendix of the description.

(Here we'll say only that an autopsy consists of examining the outside and the inside of the person to determine any pathology and, if there is doubt, the cause of death. My job was to physically help out, doing the relatively unskilled parts of the operation. But a great anatomy lesson.)

Twice or three times over the two years of this job, a half dozen student nurses would come in and sit in the balcony.   None of them fainted, but several turned green.

Working at this only in the evenings, I had some memorable experiences incidental to the work.   One example is the man who had died of terminal syphilis. The resident was freeing up the bowel, and when the appendix came loose it flipped a glob of infected fluid right past my face, luckily missing me by an inch. I wasn't wearing glasses.   There were cases that bothered even hardened me, too, that I won't describe. Mostly, though, it was just a job working on objects that no longer had people inside them.

The lab has a ghoulish reputation in a hospital. Hospitals have a labyrinth of tunnels connecting the buildings and Ancker was old even in 1946-48.   The favorite initiation of a new orderly was to give him the job of taking a shrouded body on a gurney to the lab. This would be at night, of course. And he'd be alone. In a dark part of the tunnel, the body would sit up and groan (another orderly playing the part) and the new man would show his colors. There were stories of initiates who never came back, even to pick up their paychecks. And about the "body" who chose a sloping tunnel to sit up, and who rode a runaway cart down the slope to the accompaniment of retreating footfalls. Luckily, no initiate decided to make sure that the body was really dead by whacking it.

At the end of the tunnel route was an elevator to get up to the lab. This elevator was an antique even for Ancker; it was hand-powered. There was an endless loop of rope hanging in the freight car, and you pulled on the rope on a differential pulley to slowly lift the car to the lab floor. One "body" sat up in this elevator, and the initiate spun the rope so fast that he nearly drove the car down through the floor at the bottom, and went through the wooden gate without opening it.

The tunnels were used for other sports when the work was slow. One was to take a staff member and strap him to the gurney and push him into the tunnel to where there was a leak in the roof, and to leave him there. Tunnels are great echo chambers.

Being on call, I had time on my hands often. One release was to go help my roommate, who was the X-ray technician on night call. Ancker had a really decrepit X-ray room. The big high-tension cables that looped across the top of the machine had frayed fabric covers, and the wire was exposed here and there. But the thing worked, and I got to see exactly how, because there was none of the modern sleek housing for the equipment.

My roommate had different hours than I. He was on the swing shift, going off at 11 PM. He had epilepsy with fairly well controlled seizures. But he told me how to take care of him if it happened (and it did) that he fell out of bed in a grand mal seizure. He never had seizures on the job, and his recovery time was quite rapid, but when he went, it was the full thing.

Another recreation was to help out in the receiving room, or the emergency ward. Ancker was the city-county hospital and it got the police cases, so that was interesting to say the least. It was pretty much like the TV hospital shows but with more minor injuries and more sick indigent children.

Another Bethel student and a particular friend, Cal Lundberg, was a swing shift orderly in the receiving room. Cal was well over six feet, with hands the size of a catcher's mitt. He would spread that hand over the chest of a violent patient, and say, in a deep and resonant voice, "Lie down." And they'd lie down.

In the receiving room I had a free rein to help or to leave --I wasn't an employee there, but I was a member of the hospital culture. Sometimes I was genuinely needed, such as with the big man who came in with a downward dislocation of his shoulder. Even with morphine and the curare to relax his muscles, it took three of us to hold him while a strong doctor put his knee in the man's armpit and wrenched the bone back into its socket. The man was not feeling much pain by then, but this is a particularly difficult dislocation to reduce.

I got to recognize the panting cry of a child with pneumonia, and to judge the severity of car injuries (the amount of blood isn't the clue), and to know what to expect on what night. For example, a rainy Friday night would bring in motorcyclists with abraded hips, elbows, and ears. The same sort of night would bring in elderly pedestrians, usually cut up but not seriously injured by cars. And at any time there would be the "silver fork" deformity of a Colles wrist fracture.

Bad suicide attempts (are there any good ones, come to think of it?) would come in with cut wrists. An intern on duty would sew them up, then the resident would come in and ask the patient to make a fist - and a couple of fingers would stick out. The resident would sigh and take the person up to operating to sew the severed tendons. The resident would probably emit more than a sigh at the intern when they were alone.

Head injuries are spectacular because of the blood, but if the patient was walking, they were usually superficial.

Then there was the occasional kitchen accident. Like the woman with several fingers interwoven with the beaters of her mixer. The receiving room had strong wire cutters for this, and for finger rings mashed onto the finger.

I'd tell the telephone operator where to find me when I volunteered. But to make sure, I rigged my phone with a switch that turned on a light outside my window, and I'd look for it when I was roaming. Fortunately, my room faced the inner square of the hospital.

Sometimes I'd go to the supply room, where in the evenings there was not much traffic and things were done like sharpening needles. Yes, children, in those days they sterilized and reused needles because there were not yet problems with nasty viruses that an autoclave (steam sterilizer) couldn't handle. The needles got dull, and we used fine Arkansas stone to whet them. Still, as I remember personal experience with needles of the 1940s, the ones used on me were always dull.

I didn't volunteer in the kitchen. I'd had enough of that in the Army. But I did get well acquainted with the food service staff. And I noted the size of cockroaches that inhabit hospitals.

At school, I had broken off with a girlfriend who was getting more serious than I wanted to get. Some time later her father died, and the family asked me to be present at the autopsy on their behalf. I went, of course. The pathologist wasn't nearly as thorough as we were at Ancker, but after all the issue was a simple heart attack. Afterwards I met with the family and told them the pleasant aspects of the event, assuring them that the body had been treated respectfully.

In early 1948, having realized that I was not going to get into medical school after failing a course in chemical quantitative analysis, I revised my educational plans. By then I could see that I'd need to finish my BA and spend a year or two getting a Master's degree in psychology. I told the Veteran's Administration that I'd like to go back on the GI Bill scholarship, and the VA obliged. In fact, they paid me the back support, tuition and maintenance, which I would have been getting. So I was rich. Over a thousand dollars, which was *real* money in those days. I spent some of it.

I bought a motor scooter, a red, three horsepower Cushman, and became mobile. I bought an engagement ring, the best I could afford and with the biggest diamond I'd ever held in my hand. I finished my first year at the University.

This job of pathology attendant, a subsidized learning experience for me, lasted for two years. Then came September of 1948, the hottest for some decades before and with none hotter since. In one swoop I got married and quit the job. Commuting from Minneapolis to a night job, even with the Cushman scooter that was then our "family car," was too much for a newlywed and a University student. The F grade in quantitative analysis had ended my medical school aspirations, as I mentioned earlier, so some of the relevance of the job had ended.

And someone else fell into the best work deal a student could have.

APPENDIX TO "PATHOLOGY ATTENDANT"
The "Assistance with autopsies" part of the job

(Note: if you're at all squeamish, skip this section. But in order to make sense of my job, I'll have to describe the routine. It may help to use the rationale that I used: it's just a body, there is no one living in it anymore.)

An external examination would be made of the body, and the pathologist would step on a foot switch and start his dictation. "The body is that of a mature white male about 60 years of age. The body is well nourished. Post mortem rigidity is present, and there is post mortem lividity (the pooling of blood on the back, indicating that the person died in that position, a significant indicator to a coroner). The mouth is edentulous. There is a healed surgical scar on the abdomen, with no other distinguishing marks..." and so on. Then we would proceed with the post itself.

The "Dr. Noble routine" was dear to the heart of morticians. When Ancker got done with a post the mortician had a reliable and clean field to work with. The body cavity would be clean, and stumps left of the femoral, carotid, and brachial arteries for embalming. If there had been a head post, there would be no cosmetic damage.

You start with an incision to the chest wall, from in front of one armpit down to the bottom of the rib cage, across, and up to in front of the other armpit. The flap would be freed from the bare rib cage and laid back. Then an incision would be made on the midline to the pubis, and the flaps laid back. Then the sternum would be sheared away at the costal margins (where rib bone turns into cartilege), and lifted out. Now the body cavity would be fully open and inspected. The pathologist would dictate his observations.

The cardiac sac would be opened and examined, and the heart lifted out and severed. The heart would be placed on the sectioning board and opened and examined in detail. The pathologist would then dictate his observations and decide whether to reserve the heart for more detailed or microscopic study.

Throughout, when it was feasible, blunt dissection would be used. That is, instead of cutting, finger force would be applied to free up the organs. This resulted in the separation following natural lines, with minimum ragged edges and stumps. You might call this kind of technique "dividing nature at its joints." Morticians like that, plus it gives a cleaner organ to examine.

Next came the lungs. On the sectioning board, the pathologist would slice the lungs every half-inch and inspect each slice for pathology. To section the organs, an old amputating knife would be used. This is an 11-inch blade, hollow ground like an old straightedge razor and nearly as sharp. (I still have one of those blades, and if pressed I'll describe why they're that shape.) You could tell farmer's lungs from a city dweller's by the color; there'd be black specks throughout and the knife would grit through a city lung. Again the pathologist would dictate his findings and set the remains aside in a tray.

Then the stomach and esophagus would be freed up and removed, and opened. This routine would be followed for the other organs.

My job up to now would be mostly to provide and remove trays and tools. Then, when the intestines were to be removed, I'd maintain tension on the free end as the gut was cut free along its length. But if there was a new resident, I'd have the task of showing him how to use the gut knife. Removing the intestine from the mesentery calls for a "touch" with both the knife and the folds of the mesentery. The trick is to leave minimal stump and yet avoid cutting into the intestine. You handle the gut knife like you'd handle a violin bow.

Then I'd take the intestines over to the sink and slit them open, cleaning them out for the pathologist's inspection.

If there was a "head post," then we had to take out the brain. To do this you first cut the scalp from behind one ear, over the rear of the crown, and to behind the other ear. This way the mortician can hide the incision in the hair and no distressing evidence of the post mortem exam is seen. Then the scalp is peeled forward and backward to expose the skull. A saw cut is than made behind the forehead and another across the rear of the crown, taking out somewhat more than a quarter-sphere of skull. Then the pathologist cradles the brain in one hand and gently pulls it out and back, and then reaches behind it and cuts first the optic nerves and then the brain stem. He slips the cerebellum forward past its supporting membrane and lifts the brain onto the sectioning board.

Then the brain is sectioned with that amputating knife, with each slice examined for pathology.

I usually managed to be where I could watch this sectioning closely, and occasionally was allowed to do some non-critical cuts. We'd look at and discuss such interesting parts as the lateral geniculate nuclei. The whole thing would look just like an anatomy illustration.

Now, what do you do with a brain, especially after it has been sliced? It is at best a slippery thing to handle. Well, you do with it the same thing you do with the other organs: when the post is all done, you put everything higgledy-piggledy back in the body cavity and sew it up.

The mortician will undo your stitches and take out the organs and soak them in embalming fluid. Makes you think of the mortuary practices of the ancient Egyptians, with the Pharoah's organs separately stored in canopic jars.

While the body was open, the pathologist would reach into the thigh and snip out a tiny sample of the psoas minor muscle, for some research project on muscle function.

Then the pathologist and the resident would leave and I'd put the body back together by cramming all the organs into the cavity and sewing it up.

Then I'd put the body into the colubarium and clean up the autopsy room. I'd wash and store the instruments, wash up myself, and go to supper.

CENSUS ENUMERATOR
1949

It was the spring of 1949. I had graduated from the University with a BA in the Psychology of Individual Differences. To put that to use, I'd have to get an MA, and that wouldn't begin until the fall. Time to get a full time job. My wife Bernice had been, and continued to be, employed as a cashier at Dayton's downtown. She had been earning more than came in from my GI Bill stipend; all through our marriage, the two of us leap-frogged and combined to bring home the bacon.

I'm not sure where I got the information that the job was available, but I applied for the job of census Enumerator, and got it. This was a federal civil service job. A crew of us was to take the 1948 Census of Business. There were, as I recall, about 20 of us. Our territory was the Twin City metro area.

I was mobile. I had my Cushman scooter. The others had cars of various kinds, and at least one used a motorcycle.

We each were given a census book, a big folder about 12 by 18 inches, and an assigned territory. Mine were mostly downtown Minneapolis. For example, one of my territories was the strip defined by Marquette Avenue, Seventh Street, Portland, and Ninth Street. That one included the Sexton Building on the east and the Foshay Tower on the west.

We canvassed every door in every building, going into every street and alley. We were looking for businesses of any kind. We would go in and ask about the operation. The first thing was to find out if it was a manufacturing business, because we weren't gathering information beyond identification for them. For other businesses, we asked details that businesses don't usually want to tell.

Once in a while, a business owner would refuse to talk about his business. In all except one case, I was able to convince the owner, with the credentials furnished to us, that the information would be absolutely confidential. In that one case, I said, "Look. I'm going to continue on around the block, and come back here. Meanwhile, why don't you call your lawyer and ask him what he thinks of it?" When I got back, the man was friendly and talkative.

Some of the people I visited were talkative even when it wasn't necessary. On First Avenue I found the offices of the Gorham Press. Since it was a publisher, it was a manufacturer and hence it was exempt from detailed questioning. But the man was friendly and I was interested, so I spent an hour of government time listening to him. The Gorham Press was a publisher of a kind I hadn't known existed. They published the gambling odds on team sports and related things. Gambling was illegal and it couldn't be done in Minnesota, but there was no law against developing and publishing gambling information. I learned all sorts of ins and outs of the gambling business, so much so that I left my scooter at the parking meter beyond the time for parking, and found a ticket on it -- the only moving violation ticket I've had in my life -- because it was in a zone that was no-parking from 4 to 6 PM. (In later years, I heard an echo of Gorham Press when their chief team odds maker came to me for vocational counseling; that's another story.)

In another area, the Midway, I came across the offices of Univac. Again, as a manufacturer, they were exempt from questioning but they gave me a tour anyway. Computers were remote oddities then, and the idea was new to me. They showed me things I didn't understand, but one item stood out. That was the memory drum. It was a fairly large cylinder of precision aluminum, maybe four feet long and covered with a layer of red iron oxide. I knew about magnetic memory from the then-new wire and tape recorders. This big drum was a wonder that held maybe 6/1,000,000ths of 1 percent of the hard drive of the computer on which this is typed, but it was the biggest non-volatile, random-access memory available anywhere in the world.

At an office in the Sexton Building on Portland Avenue, I was shown an electric typewriter with a memory. This memory was on punched tape. The text was typed on an IBM typewriter, which also punched the tape. The tape was then run through a reader where electrical contacts made through the holes actuated a mechanical typer. Wires from the typer went up through holes in a table to jerk down on the keys of a second typewriter, duplicating the text. This marvel of the office could duplicate form letters and allow a live typist to type in such things as addresses and salutations. Remember, the Xerox machine was yet to be invented, and carbon copies were pretty limited, so this was a great machine. Unfortunately it didn't penetrate the market before it was made obsolete by other inventions.

Being an Enumerator was not all a matter of technological exploration. It also was being out in all kinds of weather, trying to keep the book dry and trying to not drown in the rain myself. A scooter offers no shelter. But every day was an adventure. Some of my territories were in primarily residential areas with small businesses. The job was a real eye-opener for a country boy with no business experience, because business owners would answer questions about all sorts of nuts and bolts of running a business. I got to understand large and small businesses.

In a small office suite on Nicollet Avenue I ran across a company called Investors Diversified Services, later to go by its initials, IDS. Because this was the headquarters, I got to find out all of the company operations, and went away with all sorts of information but no real grasp of its meaning and above all of its future potential. And in the Sexton Building, I interviewed a manager of Minnesota Mining and Manufacturing, but didn't understand what it was all about, either. Naivete dies hard.

In the Foshay Tower, I got to go around every floor and see every office. That included the top floor, the studios of the infant TV industry. The Tower was the tallest building in Minneapolis, so the antennas were on top. I was given a tour of the very top rooms with their observation windows.

I got to know the Marquette-7th-Portland-9th tract quite well. I had almost finished it when my scooter was stolen while I had lunch. The scooter was soon recovered, but the Enumerator's book in its "trunk" was never found. I had to do most of the tract over again, faster this time because I had already covered it but slowed down by my having to sometimes explain why I was back. There never was any criticism for my having lost the book. My bet is that my boss didn't report it, so as not to have to spend several days filling out forms and maybe getting criticized himself for letting one of his men lose it.

I was fast and accurate, I found out, at least by comparison to the others. Some of them had got their jobs by pull and they didn't break a sweat in doing the work. So, when the work was cut back near the end of summer I was one of the few who were kept on to finish the job.

The whole city of Anoka was made my territory. That took about a month of going over every street and alley in the city. My route to work was thus over 30 miles long, and my scooter could make a top speed of just under 45 mph. I could make the trip in 45 minutes from

South Minneapolis. My route took me through downtown, north on Lyndale out of town, and along the West River Road to Champlain and then across the bridge into Anoka. I wore a groove in the pavement, and got to know exactly how to go into every turn in the road, how close to cut it, and how much to lean. Anoka, too, was an education. You get to know the mechanics of a city by doing that kind of census.

Then the fall came and I had to go back to school at the end of September. So I quit the job just before the work was finished, I think to the satisfaction of both the government and myself.

TEACHING ASSISTANT I
1949 to 1950

In the year 1949-50 I was a full time student in the Master of Arts program of the University's Department of Psychology.

As a full time grad student I was integrated into the culture of the Psychology Department by being appointed as a 1/4 time employee of the University as a Teaching Assistant or TA. Even in those days a lot of the work of a University was done by TAs rather than by professors.

I helped professors with their research projects, I was a resource to students whose questions didn't require the professor's intervention, I graded papers, and I helped to teach the laboratory sections of courses.

As a laboratory assistant I accompanied the professors to the lectures and I met with the classes when they did their lab work. In psychology, the lab work consisted then of things like giving each other the hearing or vision tests, or designing questionnaires and surveys. I have no idea what psychology students do in labs these days, but that was nearly a half- century nearer in time to the experimental psychologists who investigated sensation and perception at the turn of century.

In grading the lab reports I got my most severe tests of my own competence. It was also where I learned to read almost any handwriting. However, I had to give a failing grade to a friend (Bill Fenderson) whose handwriting was totally illegible. I kept telling him that I couldn't read it and would he please print, but he must have been a fatalist.

No, come to think of it, my most severe test was when Dave Lykken and I were assigned to grade the final exam of Physiological Psychology, because we were the only two TAs who had taken the course. The professor was Starke Hathaway, who had written the book in the same prose he used in his lectures. "To recapitulate the cerebellar connections: there are, first, incoming fibers through the pons from ultimate sources chiefly concerned with proprioception..." And Hathaway didn't use only multiple choice test items, for which he could provide a scoring key; he used open-ended questions and short essays. Somehow, Dave and I got by on that one.

Being a TA made me part of the Departmental culture in a way that is difficult for anyone in modern education to grasp. The Department was a social unit as well as a work unit. Although we TAs were peasants we were integrated with the mighty ones. The highlight was the annual staff party. There was the dignified Chairman, Richard Elliot, in a stovepipe hat and lecturing on mythical shore birds while two assistant professors produced the birdcalls on Galton pipes. And I was chosen to lampoon my major advisor, Donald Gildersleeve Paterson, by lying on a couch and singing a homemade version of "All Pooped Out" in a fake Swedish dialect while another TA pulled yards of tangled wires out of my shirt (the diagnosis was that I had my wires crossed). To this day, sometimes when I read of the exploits of some famous psychologists, I say to myself, "I was a TA with him!"

The year of being TA helped our finances because the terms of my Federal stipend didn't forbid that kind of employment. It also helped my academic endeavors. We TAs formed a joint study group in which each of us made special study of one of the broad subjects that made up the preliminary written examination for the doctorate. Well, it helped me, but not enough. I stayed on the MA track, completing my course work and deferring my research paper until after becoming a Rehabilitation Counselor.

With the course work completed, and a paper to write that took three years to complete, I moved out of academia into the semi-cruel world of civil service.

VOCATIONAL REHABILITATION COUNSELOR
AND SUPERVISOR
The first professional job
1950 to 1957

In the spring of 1950 I was completing my MA in Counseling Psychology at the University.

(I had gone to Bethel Junior College for a semester in 1942, went into the Army, returned to Bethel in 1946, and graduated with my AA in 1947. Then on to the University for a BA. I intended a pre-med curriculum, but then I failed (chemical) Quantitative Analysis, so I switched to Differential Psychology. In the fall of 1949, with a wife partly supporting me and with the GI Bill doing the rest, I went on for a year's classes in Counseling Psychology, with D. G. Paterson as my major advisor.)

D. G. Paterson was a phenomenon. He was the only full professor at the U, that I knew of, who didn't have a Ph D. He didn't need one. He was one of the original Army psychologists who, in 1918 or thereabouts, invented group testing of individuals. He was a major author of the 1918 Army Beta, a non-paper test of intelligence. Later, he was the author of most of the personnel tests used in industry in the 1940s and '50s: the Minnesota Rate of Manipulation, the Minnesota Clerical Test, the Paper Form Board, and some lesser tests.

Pat (no one called him Donald Gildersleeve Paterson to his face) was a no-nonsense, practical psychologist. I learned from him that, if you couldn't see a statistical relationship by inspecting the data, it was probably too small to have practical significance. He always drew up his data on charts before he ran statistical tests, and he didn't bother to run the tests if the data didn't show what he could do with the results. This is a technique that you can use if you are a pioneer, where you are investigating pioneering matters; fine-grained statistics are for situations where the big picture is known, and you are looking for subtle details. He was person- as well as personnel-oriented. He would ask of a new screening test, "How many people will it wrongly screen out? How many will it wrongly screen in?" If the trade-offs were not worth it, he wouldn't let it fly.

He was also the man from whom I learned the Barnum Effect. He used to give his sophomores a long personality questionnaire, telling them that one of the graduate students wanted to try it out. He warned the students not to take it too seriously, because it was still experimental. The test would have the usual embarrassing questions. Then he'd take the answer sheets in for scoring, and come back with sealed, individual interpretations. He'd ask the students to rate how accurately the test had analyzed their personalities, and almost all would report that it had them dead to rights. Then, next class period, he'd report the ratings they'd given the test, and he'd ask for a brave volunteer to read his own interpretation sheet to the class, and it would gradually dawn upon them that everyone had been given the exact same interpretation. Pat would say, "Let that be a lesson to you. I gleaned the statements that describe your personalities from astrology books and weight-and-fortune-for-a-penny machines. There's one born every minute." I never forgot that lesson as I did my own diagnoses in later years, and when I read other psychologist's reports.

Pat was also directive. He didn't believe that anyone should pretend to be a counselor unless he knew more about the subject than the counselee. Why go to someone who would "draw the answer out of you" if he wasn't an expert? So Pat was directive with me, and never told me why he gave his command.

"They're giving a test for state Vocational Rehabilitation Counselors in St. Paul next week. Be there." So I went, and passed the test, and took the job. It paid professional wages -- $244.00 a month.

I later learned that Pat had trained Don Dabelstien, the person who became the national leader in rehabilitation in 1943, and who made the state-federal agency into the first actual system operation of government. That is, Dabelstien worked out a system analytic structure for accounting for the progress of a client through the service system, with explicit blocks of action, documented decision points, and defined outcome statuses. Entering professional life in that system has shaped my system outlook, even if I had to make my own flow chart of the process. People weren't using flow charts in 1950, much less the 1940s, but Dabelstien thought in systems analytic terms, as do I.

(That's why my business card always carried the superimposed systems analytic symbols for action/decision/documentation. That was my business logo for many years.)

My first month as Counselor in the State Division of Vocational Rehabilitation (DVR) was orientation to agency procedures and trips with experienced counselors to see how it was done. The job was an integration of professional and bureaucratic operations, with the Dabelstien system forming the framework of the professional activity.

There were 16 people who formed the professional and administrative staff of DVR. I turned out to be the first trained psychologist in the agency since 1943. Up to my joining the agency, there had been no psychologists since Dabelstien. The counselors and administrators were mostly former school principals and superintendents. This made me, in some ways, the lead maverick in the agency. Not that I was in conflict, but my ways of analyzing things were slightly different.

I was assigned to the Minneapolis office, which was responsible for the band of counties across the middle of the state. There were other offices in St. Paul, Mankato and Duluth. My personal assigned beat was the city of Minneapolis itself, except for the work being done within the public schools by two counselors who had mixed DVR-school identity. I had all handicapped people in Minneapolis over age 21 in my caseload, except for those served by the State Services for the Blind.

The District Supervisor, Ed Berhow, was a very pleasant and older man who had been a school principal. He dropped me into the caseload gently, and showed me the ropes. I would have three months until the next quarterly caseload report was due.

Our office was on the eighth floor of the Metropolitan Building in downtown Minneapolis. This building was the first steel framework building west of Chicago, and was contemporary with (1891) and externally similar to the old Court House that still stands. The external walls were red sandstone blocks, 16 feet thick at the bottom and rising like a castle to ramparts and tower above the 12th floor. Internally the Metropolitan Building was a marvel. The framework was set around wrought iron columns trimmed with semi-Corinthian leaves. In the center was a courtyard that was open from the skylight roof to the first floor and it was ringed with a wrought iron railing topped with a three-inch brass rail. Between the railing and the offices arrayed around the outside walls were translucent glass floors, where you could see the soles of the shoes of people walking above you. The elevators, with human operators who swung long levers, were open-work wrought iron cages, riding on cables in open-work wrought iron shafts.

One of the elevator operators was Walfred Lund, a well-aged man from Mora, Minnesota. He spoke with a thick Skåning accent, because a lot of the settlers of Mora were from the Swedish province of Skåne. Some years into my service in the Metropolitan Building, my wandering brother Stanley came in from Morocco to see me. When Walfred, who had no idea of who he was, asked what floor Stan wanted, Stan recognized his accent and said to him "Öksaskaft!" and Walfred dissolved in laughter, because "öxaskaft," meaning "axehandle," is the punch line of a standard Skåning joke.

Some of my clients wouldn't ride those elevators because they were afraid to rise up eight floors in anything so exposed to the open air. So I'd have to go down to the main floor and walk up the stairs with them, or interview them at the lunch counter. Fortunately, most of the people saw nothing unusual in the elevator setup.

I inherited my first cases. Then I began to get new applicants of my own.

The first step was to determine whether they were eligible for our service. The criteria were: a disability established by medical report; the evidence that, for this person, the disability constituted a vocational handicap; and the determination that competitive employment was a feasible outcome if we gave service. If the problem was psychological I did the testing and had it reviewed by our medical consultant in the state office. I, as counselor, made the other determinations and documented them. If the person was eligible, we would proceed.

The next step was the vocational diagnosis. In this, we would interview and test to determine the potentials, and review history and the present options. With the client, we would then settle upon a vocational goal.

It might be a good idea to describe here my idea of what counseling should be. I've already noted the directive stance of my MA advisor. As I formulated to myself the proper nature of counseling, it was: counseling is helping the client to understand himself, his motivations, and his abilities; to understand the options open to him; to choose for himself the goal among those options; to undertake a course of action to reach his goal; and to persist to success. Counseling is done by talking and relating, and in our situation by developing much of the information needed by the client to choose and succeed.

To help the client to reach his goal we had three options: correct, compensate, or circumvent. In other words, simply fix the problem, make up for it, or get around it. Actually, the agency did not analyze its capability in that way; the "three Cs" was my own invention, implicit at first and only written into the professional literature a couple of decades later by those to whom I taught it and who credited me for it. But it worked this way.

The first choice would be to *correct* the disability. For example, we bought artificial limbs for a number of people who could then return to work. In some instances, we (the DVR agency) paid for elective surgery. Very rarely, because it was not too common in those days, we paid for therapy. But if we could fix the disability, that was the route to go.

The second, and the most frequently used, was to *compensate*. Since the disability was a vocational disadvantage to the person, we would provide the means for the person to get a compensatory advantage. Our most popular tool was vocational training, since a trained person could compensate using that strength.

The third choice was *circumvention*. Actually, almost all of our vocational counseling included the application of this strategy. Since our clients had residual disabilities, our task was to help them find occupations or work sites where we could circumvent (get around) the resulting vocational handicap. For example, a machine operator who lost a left hand, and who had the talent, might circumvent the disability by becoming an accountant, where he would not need to do two-handed manipulation. To use the circumvention strategy, we usually had to give other services such as training to implement it. But occasionally, we could through counseling directly find a job that got around the disability without any further service; but then we had to document the fact that we had done something useful and not just capitalized on random events.

Counseling and guidance were the core of our work, at least for me. For some of the older counselors, a more immediate approach was taken, that of routinely providing training in one of the popular fields (clerical work and shoe repair) without much consideration of other options.

Because the other DVR personnel were not psychologists, I was sometimes asked to test applicants who were mentally retarded. I was not asked to test mentally ill applicants, of course, because that would require a psychiatric opinion for the diagnosis. Even for mentally retarded applicants, our psychiatric consultant was not sure of my competence for a while.

The tests I used were of all levels, ranging from the paper aptitude tests that could be used by any clerk to the clinical instruments that were restricted to use by qualified professionals. I administered and interpreted individual intelligence tests like the Wechsler-Bellevue, projective tests like the Thematic Apperception Test, diagnostic tests like the Bender Motor Gestalt, and personality tests like the Minnesota Multiphasic Personality Inventory. For a while, I was the only counselor in the agency who was qualified to do that.

In 1953, prodded by my MA advisor, I finished the paper for my MA degree. I was working under a thinly-veiled threat by the American Psychological Association and by the State of Minnesota, both of whom were moving toward a requirement of the Ph D in psychology to grant their credentials: from the APA, full membership; from the State Board of Examiners of Psychologists, certification as a psychologist. I got the degree and was grandfathered by both organizations. When I became a Certified Psychologist in 1953, there were fewer than 200 psychologists in the state. When in later years I became a Licensed Psychologist and later a Licensed Consulting Psychologist, my original certificate number of 194 continued to identify me as one of the pioneers. In getting my original membership and certificate I don't doubt that it helped to be able to list my advisor, D. G. Paterson, as a reference.

In the course of my work I had contacts with schools, businesses who gave on-the-job training, artificial limb makers, and medical facilities.

Of the several artificial limb makers in Minneapolis, the largest was the Trautman shop about 5 blocks from our office. At first my contacts were by phone and by mailing authorizations, but over time I became familiar with the working floors of the shops. One image that remains was the multiple-spindle duplicating carver in the Trautman shop, with a model artificial foot having its contours duplicated on an array of maple blocks. At Trautman's also, early work was done on Fiberglas and resin and I got interested. I begged a pint of Bakelite C8 resin, the forerunner of the polyester resin that (with Fiberglas reinforcement) "Fiberglas" boats are made out of. That allowed me to get a few years' head start on other hobbyists working in Fiberglas.

The job of a DRV counselor was not highly structured. In the course of my duties, anything that would further the caseload or the cause was fair game. I early got involved in the nationally initiated "Employ the Handicapped" week each October. After the first couple of years I was made chairman of the Mayor's Committee on Employment of the Handicapped, the group that was responsible for local promotion and publicity. This led to my being featured in the Star-Tribune as a "Good Neighbor of the Week," complete with picture. The reporter who was sent to interview me was an older man whose usual beat was feature writing, and he decided to write a fluffy piece, and I have to live with it.

By the standards of our agency I wasn't very productive in my caseload. That is, over the years, fewer of my clients got jobs quickly. I wasn't very good for the bottom line. Looking back I can see that I was too easily side-tracked into dealing with issues that were not central to the person's employability. I did a lot of personal counseling, and I'd aggressively follow up on people who would be left to drop off the caseload by other counselors. I was not a good bureaucrat, except that I did make good case notes -- and a bureaucrat who had documentation was immune from administrative criticism. And I did interesting work.

There was Irene. She first came in with her parents to apply for rehabilitation because she'd been in the Hastings State Hospital. There everyone got the diagnosis of paranoid schizophrenia, so that's the label she came with, but it didn't take much of a psychologist to see that she wasn't schizoid. She was about 19 years old, I think. She seemed to me, intuitively, to be a "dry alcoholic," one who wasn't using alcohol but who otherwise acted like one. Both she and her parents assured me that she wasn't drinking, so I mentally marked her down as having that kind of personality. Anyhow, I interviewed her and found that she didn't believe that she had a problem. So I told her bluntly but kindly that I couldn't help people who didn't have problems, but that I'd be glad to see her when she did have one.

A year later, Irene was back. She had a problem; she couldn't get a job. I bent some rules, though I used them literally the way the book said I should. Since she had that schizophrenia diagnosis, and because she was unemployed because of her ill-defined inability to get and keep a job, I declared her eligible. Then I worked on the case. We went through the standard steps of vocational diagnosis, and cosmetology was within her ability and she wanted to be in that line of work. Fine. I authorized her tuition, and continued counseling. I sweated blood on that case.

Irene completed beautician training, with occasional dropouts. I still saw her for counseling to keep her going. Then she needed minor surgery, and I authorized that. Then she began to have disastrous relationships with older men, and each time she claimed to have learned her lesson. She had some bizarre emotional episodes, and we worked through them. She was on her own now, not living with her parents, and moving too often. I ended up with 22 pages of case notes on her, the most I'd ever had. And then she got married, and I had to close the case with her employed as homemaker instead of beautician. Well, the agency was satisfied, the case was satisfactorily closed and the agency got credit for a rehabilitation.

Some 25 or 30 years later, I got a call from Irene. She was in town visiting, and could I see her? I sure could. Then she told me that her marriage had turned out OK, but that she'd been fooling me all the time I was working with her; she *was* an alcoholic during those years (she'd been dry for well over a decade when we met again). But my unfailing trust in her, misplaced as it was, had kept her going. Thinking back, I don't think that things would have turned out as well if I hadn't been so trusting and naive.

Irene illustrates another of my foibles. In my zeal for confidentiality, I not only refused to discuss cases with friends and spouse, but I erased names from my memory when I didn't need them. For years I tried to remember Irene's name, and couldn't. Then she phoned, and memory clicked in.

You may wonder how a case could pile up 22 pages of notes. You see, we had to dictate notes on every contact with the client, whether an interview was in the office, a home visit, or a contact with a school or employer. Those notes would enable the case to be transferred to another counselor without missing a beat.

We actually dictated in those days. At first the secretary would take the dictation in shorthand and type the notes. After some three years we got dictating machines, Grundigs that used floppy plastic disks and cut a groove like any other record, and the secretary would play it back and type it. In the world of the 2000s, an agency couldn't afford that much secretarial help and those of us who use computers would prefer to do our own work. Those professionals who don't use computers now have a short vocational life ahead of them. But this was the 1950s.

Another client, Peter. He was about 55 years old, and every few years he'd come to the rehab office and apply. His artificial leg would be worn out. Peter was philosophical about his amputation, claiming that it was easier for him to fish through the ice in the winter because only one foot would get cold. So we'd dredge up the old file, go through the routine of establishing his eligibility, and buy him a leg. Then he'd go out and get a job and the agency would get credit for another disabled person returned to employment. But Peter was a tramp at heart, a good-hearted soul who worked as little as possible, and he'd be back in another five or six years. It was worth it.

Andy was another client I'll long remember. He had epilepsy, and his seizures were only moderately controlled. But his big problem as that he was a simple paranoid who had systematic delusions of persecution. He had a long record of being so difficult that most counselors wouldn't even consider him. It was he who showed me how to deal with a simple paranoid (not a paranoid schizophrenic, where I never had any success). When he told me what his enemies were up to, I didn't contradict him. I agreed that it might be possible, and what could we do that would help him to function anyway? He got so that he could count on my not arguing delusions with him, and we got along fine. He even got a job.

Another psychiatric type where I had some success in vocational counseling was the psychopathic personality, the classic Minnesota (theoretical, not geographic, construct) "Pd." A simple psychopath doesn't feel pain in advance, and without anticipating that he'll be sorry, he does things like commit crimes. He doesn't have a feeling for the distress of others, either. So he's dangerous and he gets punished. I'd know that I was dealing with a psychopath when I found myself liking the person on the basis of not enough contact -- too much charm. The case history, and/or the Minnesota Multiphasic Personality Inventory, would identify the type. The successful tactic that I found was to be frank about their status, and they would almost always acknowledge that that's why they were always in trouble. So, since most of them were bright enough, I'd counsel them to use their reasoning power instead of the missing "instinct" to avoid trouble. Mostly, it worked. At least, I had several successful cases of that kind. It turns out that I was using what later became known as "rational-emotive therapy."

Most of my cases, though, were simple ones of a physical disability that we could circumvent or compensate or both. A man in a manual occupation would lose an arm, for example. We'd test and counsel and find that he could cope with a non-manual occupation, bookkeeping or radio technician, for example, and we'd authorize the training. Usually the choice would work out and the school would find the job. The agency built its reputation on that kind of case.

The tests we used were the ones that had been designed for personnel purposes, which means that they were better at telling us what the person couldn't do than what he could do. But on the strength of my psychological training under Pat himself, I could use tests in a more discriminating fashion, and even steer some clients away from formal testing because I knew that the result would be a "false negative" -- a wrong score that said that he couldn't do the job, when I knew he could.

In the early 1950s a new test battery was put to use in the State Employment Agencies and used by our agency on referral. This was the General Aptitude Test Battery, or GATB. When it came into use I noted some peculiar patterns of result. For one thing, all our tuberculosis ex-patients scored as not meeting the standard minimum pattern for any occupation. And the other tests that I'd given the clients weren't so pessimistic.

I wrote to the Federal agency that had supplied the GATB, and tried to get its norms. The answers were not very explicit. (But our agency's Director in St. Paul learned that I'd been corresponding with Washington, and he got all wrought up, imagining that I was part of a plot to get him fired. I wouldn't have been unhappy if he were to leave, but that wasn't what I was doing.) The norms were just not forthcoming.

I undertook some research within the agency. I got the scores of all our clients in the state who had taken the GATB, and plotted the profiles. It turned out that the two sub-tests of the GATB that were most important to the two occupational channels into which we steered most of our clients, clerical and light mechanical, were the lowest points for our clients. This made no sense. And still none of the TB clients met any of the minimum occupational profiles. So I circulated a memo warning our counselors to not let the GATB screen out clients without considering other evidence.

About those TB clients: the usual treatment for TB in those days before drugs was to put the person on extended bed rest. This made them pretty slow when they "got out," and the GATB is a short-sample, timed test. No wonder they scored poorly. As to the other clients with poor scores, the same demand of the GATB that the person make rapid shifts among different kinds of tasks was too daunting to people who had not worked for a while.

A few years later, when the next version of the GATB came out, there was a manual with published norms. And then the grapevine told me why I hadn't been able to get the norms for the first version. It seems that the two people who had developed the GATB for the Federal government had been trained in psychology in Minnesota, and they had been under such time pressure to finish the test that they didn't have respectable norm groups. They had used as few as five people to norm some sub-tests! And they had made up the distributions on which the scores were based. Fortunately, they had guessed right. When proper norming was done on the second version of the GATB, the B002, the score patterns turned out essentially the same as had been made up by Shartle and Dvorak. And because there were no norms they could give me, my correspondents in Washington had been evasive.

I did some other research on the job. My MA thesis was to investigate the cases that were successfully closed as rehabilitated versus the cases that were unsuccessful. The answer to that question was not encouraging: the determining difference was whether the counselor had actually seen the client before determining eligibility and providing service. I had to leave out the identification of the culprits, but I knew that two of the counselors who worked in the Minneapolis Schools had simply accepted all handicapped students who were referred, and had counted on most of them becoming employed after leaving school. Then the agency would get credit for their rehabilitation, having actually done nothing. Almost all the unsuccessful cases were the students who didn't get work in those caseloads; if they did find work, the cases were successful.

Another interesting case was Arthur. His left arm had been amputated above the elbow, and he had being provided by our agency with seminary training to be a Lutheran minister. After a while, trouble arose. He was a good student, and there was no doubt of his Christian life and his theological soundness. However, the leaders of his synod came to the conclusion that, while he could get the training all right, he could not become ordained as a minister. They looked up the Levitical prohibition against any "maimed" man being a priest, and cited the more practical problem that he could not hold a communion plate in his left, mechanical hook hand. I went round and round with those synod leaders. I wrote and I called (so did Arthur), until finally the objection narrowed down to one fact: he couldn't hold that communion plate in a mechanical hook and not give his parishioners the willies.

We took this problem up with the local artificial limb companies. The Realastic artificial hand had just come on the market. This was a soft plastic skin that fitted over the functional artificial hand, and was complete to fingernails, fingerprints, and knuckle hair. We got them to make up a hand for Arthur, and to fill it with microcrystaline wax around a malleable silver wire frame. Now he could flip up his forearm, lock the elbow with a button, and rotate the wrist to a plate-holding pose, then slip the plate into a hand that he'd formed into the right grasp. It took a little more struggle with the synod, but we got him ordained.

(Thirty years later, I found his name as the pastor of the Rush Lake Lutheran Church, and drove out of my way home from our cabin to see him. He was then looking forward to retirement.)

In 1955, my District Supervisor Ed Berhow retired. That left a vacancy in the position and I naturally applied. At that time I had not yet learned that I'm not supervisory material, and I felt that I had earned the promotion. In civil service terms, I had indeed earned it, being a veteran, well educated, and with five years of longevity in the job in that district. The powers that were in St. Paul did promote me, probably against their better judgment.

Now I was responsible for not only my old job (I wasn't immediately replaced, and continued to carry a caseload), but also for the other counselors and staff. When I took the job, in the middle of 1955, there were four counselor positions in my district. In the next few months the expansion of rehabilitation that took place in 1955-56 increased our office staff, one counselor at a time.

The State office didn't like having to promote me, and so they sent to my district all the new counselors who looked like they would be unproductive or troublesome.

I already had a couple of strange counselors whom I inherited from Ed Berhow. One was John (not his real name), who was so compulsive that he'd spend much of his days tracing and retracing the writing of his case notes. He was the one counselor who never did get the hang of dictating notes. When we got dictating machines, I thought that he'd be able to do his work that way, since you can sit with the machine idle while you collect your thoughts. Not John. He still worked with a

74

pencil, and his case folders were almost black with retraced writing. He didn't get much work done, but he was a nice guy and under civil service rules, it was impossible to fire him.

Then there was Ernie, one of our best counselors and the only person whom I've ever seen who was able to counsel true schizophrenics. Ernie would sit at his desk with a client (most of our counselors didn't have private offices at that point) and the two of them would make sort of chirping noises at each other, and he got those people rehabilitated. Ernie left after a couple of years to enter medical school, and I think that he became a psychiatrist. If he did, he's good at his trade.

The Minneapolis District got new counselors, because we were in the nationwide expansion of Vocational Rehabilitation that took place in the mid-50s.

We got Jack Richardson -- Dirty Jack, as we called him, because we were into affectionate nicknames in those days. Jack was bright and almost hyperactive, and he gave the state office fits. In his first six months, until he got civil service tenure, I had to go over to St. Paul every week or so to persuade the central office not to fire Jack. They never did understand him but he was one of the best counselors we had. His clinical insight was outstanding, and he got his psychological training mostly on the job in our office.

We got Bob. He was a genuine psychopathic personality, and he'd make a great salesman, if you didn't care whom he skinned. He had a heart of gold, but no depth of feeling and he didn't anticipate consequences. He actually did things that should have gotten him fired, and cut corners in unethical ways. I never minded the cutting of corners by "my" counselors, but Bob was different. What he did off the job, by accounts that reached me, was even worse. It was a relief when he realized that he was in the wrong field and moved on.

We got Dick Henze. The state office gave him to me because they thought that he'd never amount to much. Dick is a quiet fellow who doesn't toot his own horn, but he's bright, and dedicated, and a learner. I assigned him to our Minneapolis Schools sub-office, a spot that was particularly hard to deal with, because I could see that he was a real professional, and he did fine. We later got him reassigned to the District office.

We got Del Cahoon - Delwin D. Cahoon. He was from Askov, MN and one of the brightest men I've known. He had talents coming out his ears. Del could forge any signature and pick any lock. I sometimes found my initials on requisitions that I'd never seen, but invariably they were ones I would have signed. But Del was skilled and dedicated to doing a good job, and he prospered. After a couple of years he returned to the University to get his doctorate. He was going to make the behavioral conditioning of a sensitive plant (*Mimosa pudica*) into a doctoral thesis, but he found that the University either was too alert to humor, or was humorless, and he changed his plan. Instead, he tested whether a counselor could steer the attention of a counselee by using minimal cues. Every time one of his clients (this was at the VA counseling center) would mention work, he'd say, "M-hm." The results showed that he could make his clients, who were chronically unemployed and uninterested in being rehabilitated, concentrate entirely upon the subject of work. He got his Ph D. What he didn't put in the thesis was the fact that not one of the clients got a job, and I'll bet he's still laughing, though he wouldn't admit that it was all a joke. He ended up as a well-known professor of psychology out east.

We got Dick Thoreson. I assigned him also to the Minneapolis Schools office, and he did well. He became one of the premier University professors in rehabilitation, in Missouri I think mostly, in the 1960s. For a couple of years he taught at the University of Reading in England. Bernice and I visited him there.

We got Roz Voelske. She was sent over from St. Paul for me to interview. When she was about due to show up -- But first you have to know about Sylvia. Sylvia was the head secretary in the state office, one of those people who was the real executive of the agency. She was a nice person, but very stiff and prudish. But back to Roz. When the time for her interview came, I went into my office to wait for her. There on the wall, Dirty Jack and Bob had posted a Playboy centerfold with the signature, "Love, Sylvia." I had just time enough to get it down when Roz walked in. Her first words were, "I suppose you won't want me to work here, because I'm only 22 and I'm a woman." She was competent, pleasant, Junoesque, and very attractive. Of course we wanted her to work there. She became one of our best counselors, only leaving after my own departure and leaving then because she got married to a Canadian.

With so many new counselors, and with such sketchy central office in-service training, I had to provide the professional orientation for our staff. I held regular staff meetings, but I also wrote a series of memos that detailed how to conduct a professional service system. Years later, the counselors who were with me during those times said that those memos were the best textbooks they'd had.

We moved to a new office on Lake Street, at Colfax Avenue. It was a hole in the wall kind of office, but we were able to divide it so that everyone had a cubicle. This was a great improvement, because we were getting a heavy caseload of difficult cases, with a large percentage of mentally retarded and mentally ill clients.

There was the dark winter morning when I came to the office a bit before our 8 o'clock opening time and found the secretary already there but huddled up in a corner. I assumed that it was the cold, but then came to the entry to my cubicle. There, reared back on its "heels" and holding a tree branch like a baseball bat, was a 5-foot red Sumatra orang utan. He was stuffed, but he was real enough to give any secretary the willies. And I knew that Jack had an 8 o'clock appointment with one of his most disturbed clients, a woman who had illusions of her priest's disembodied hand in her bed. Fortunately, a couple of other counselors came in before she arrived, and we clustered around that orang to hide it while she walked past, then we draped it. Jack and I stayed late and we carried that orang down to the basement and locked it in a steel cabinet and took the key home. No one admitted knowing anything about how the orang got there.

Next morning, the orang was gone, leaving a note that he didn't like our hospitality anyway. In the fresh snow outside were narrow-gauge tire tracks, and Dick Henze drove a small Nash Metropolitan. The cabinet lock had been picked neatly, and also Del's wife was a key-holding teaching assistant in Botany at the University, and that department was connected by tunnel to the Zoology building where a stuffed orang might be found. And both Dick and Del were dewy in their innocence. They still are.

We spun off new district offices in Fergus Falls and St. Cloud, breaking up the Minneapolis District. That reduced my load, but I had to train the people who were going to those new offices. One was Wild Bill Casey, another tiger of a counselor who would never have made it past his initial interview if we had not gotten a new state Director with more vision. He took over the Fergus Falls office.

In my capacity of District Supervisor I got to know the ins and outs of the service community. One of the episodes that I was privy to is still not well known, but I was there, and I saw it.

For a few years, the Easter Seal Society (officially, the Society for Crippled Children and Adults) had sparked its annual Easter fund drive by talking about the Minneapolis Rehabilitation Center it was going to build. This brought in money, but the public began to get impatient to see the Center. Pressure built up, and so the Executive Director of the Easter Seal Society came up with a plan. Since it was in my area I was sent over to see what to make of it. As the plan unfolded it appeared that the Society was to pay $10,000 (real money in those days) to a private owner of a light manufacturing plant to move his operation to Minneapolis and run it as a sheltered workshop. The Society guaranteed him a profit of another $10,000 each year, and the entrepreneur was to select and hire handicapped workers. And he was to do this under the Federal sheltered workshop license held by the Society. I listened to the plan, told the Director that it was illegal, and so reported to our state office.

Well, the Society went ahead anyway. They rented a building on Lake Street and began the workshop. Our office provided testing and counseling of clients. I assigned Dick Henze, our best psychologist, to it. The shop opened. The Society hired Bob Will, a man from Detroit, to run it (actually, I think, to take the fall because by then they knew that they were breaking the law). Then the Federal Labor Department investigated it, fined the Society an undisclosed large amount (though I heard what it was -- almost enough to bankrupt the Society) for violating the Minimum Wage law, and shut it down.

What came of it? Fairly quickly, Bob Will brought the Society for Crippled Children to the Kenny Institute to salvage the Society's future.

Shortly before, the Kenny Institute had decided to expand its occupational therapy department into a prevocational unit at 18th Street and Chicago Avenue. Dr. Paul Elwood, Director of the Kenny Institute, called me in to advise him how to set up a rehabilitation center. I told him what I usually told such people: I could give him an outline, but it's like building a big dam; you don't just ask for a blueprint, you hire the best engineer you can find and turn him loose. The Rehab Center hired Doug Fenderson, the smartest move they ever made, together with Al Siftar. They researched the nation's cutting edge on this technology, and quickly got a successful unit going.

Bob Will persuaded the Kenny Institute to join with the Society for Crippled Children and Adults to build a real rehabilitation center. Kenny had the land next door and the two agencies built a Taj Mahal of rehab centers. It throve for several years.

The time came for me to move on. I'd known all along that I was miscast as a supervisor. Other options opened up. For one thing, one of my professional colleagues, Lloyd Lofquist, was the Chairman of the University's Rehabilitation Counselor program, and he asked me to come over and be a student.

So I did. Bernice took over the family budget and much of its support, because my stipend as a graduate student wouldn't really cover our family's needs. And I took a half-time job as psychologist at the Opportunity Workshop. That's the next chapter.

(I took two years of graduate training in Counseling Psychology, having first tried for the doctoral program in Clinical Psychology. I failed to meet the psychometric profile for Clinical, and I'm glad; that would not have been my style. I was bright enough, but I had the wrong personality. Those two years did help my career, anyway.)

PSYCHOLOGIST, SHELTERED WORKSHOP
1958 to 1962

In 1953 and later, while I was a state Vocational Rehabilitation Counselor, I seem to have done some advisory work on the organizing and start-up of a sheltered workshop for mentally retarded youth. I say, "seem to," because I don't have any clear memory of it. But the workshop Director in later years said that I did, and that I played a major role in structuring it, so maybe it's so. That was before this chapter opened.

But at the end of 1957, when I resigned as District Supervisor of the central Minnesota region of the state agency, I went back to school. That meant that I had to find a means of financial support, and the half-time position that opened up at the Opportunity Workshop was just what was needed.

The Opportunity Workshop -- the "OpShop" -- had been founded in November of 1953, being at that time either the first or second sheltered workshop for mentally retarded youth in the country. The founder was Laura Zemlin, with substantial help from her friend Katherine Sahlin, the wife of the owner of a large construction company.

Laura had been a teacher at the Home Study School, which was a private school for the children who were too retarded to be accepted in the public schools. At that time public education was only for the so-called "educable mentally retarded," those with IQs of maybe 70 or better, who were considered to be able to profit from education. (In another context, the chapter on my work with the Minneapolis Public Schools, I'll expand upon that.)

Louise Whitbeck Frazer had established the Home Study School because her daughter Jean was mentally retarded -- that is, she couldn't learn in school. It turned out that she suffered from almost total receptive aural aphasia. That means that she could hear speech and other sounds, but couldn't make what was said to her into language and understand it. Later, she learned to read lips as well as to read text, so her intelligence otherwise was pretty good.

This is one of the data that began for me to make a distinction between mental retardation and mental deficiency. A person is mentally retarded if he is -- well, retarded. That is, if he is behind schedule in learning the tasks of life. There may be any number of reasons why the person is retarded, and one of them *may* be that he is mentally deficient -- that is, deficient in mental capacity. But the full development of this thesis took place over many years, and I only put it on paper two jobs later.

Anyhow, Mrs. Frazer got so stirred up over the schools' rejection of Jean that she decided to start a school of her own. The school she founded later became the Louise Whitbeck Frazer School, which is still operating.

Mrs. Frazer was a zealot. So was Laura Zemlin. Things like the Home Study School and the Opportunity Workshop can only be started by zealots, people who won't give in to the idea that something can't be done. So they do it. Zealots have their limitations, which show up after the thing they started against conventional wisdom becomes accepted and grows beyond what they can run themselves. Mrs. Frazer rose above this limitation of zealots; it was a problem to Laura; more on that later.

Laura's son Jim was a student at the Home Study School and he was then about 16 years old. At the same time as Jim, 14 other students were "aging out" of the school. They were no longer children. They couldn't go to work; no one would hire them, and they couldn't manage the duties of a job anyway. Some of them had very limited language; some had neurological problems that made them poorly coordinated. What to do?

The year was 1953. There were sheltered workshops where physically handicapped people could be employed at pay commensurate with their productivity, but none for mentally retarded people.

With the parents of the 15 students who were becoming too old for school, and the help of her friend Katherine, Laura bought the bungalow next door to the school (at 6300 Penn Av So, Richfield) and created a workshop. A sheltered workshop is a non-profit agency that offers, together with other services, a work setting geared to the pace and scope of the limitations that characterize its workers. They can work, but not competitively. At their best their work may be only 15% as productive as an average worker's. The best of them might be half as productive as average, some only 5%. They usually need special and extra supervision and special work layout in order to be able to work at all. And no one, in 1953, knew how to do that with mentally retarded people. Laura created it.

She first sat down with the workers (when they moved over to the bungalow, their title changed to "worker," and woe to the person who called them "students" in Laura's hearing!). They told her the work rules should be, and the next day she sat down with them again and told them that they'd made the rules too tough. They pared them down to just ten rules.

They were simple rules. The workers could say "Good morning!" to someone once when they came in, and then they couldn't greet that person a second time. That was to cure them of being a pest. They had to stay at their work stations until dismissed, but they had to leave them at break time; that cured roaming and preservation. They could not speak to visitors unless given a question; that cured distraction. They had to obey without question the directions of the volunteers who were their supervisors. They could not put their hands on anyone, at work *or* on the bus to and from work. (In those days, an obviously retarded person who pawed a stranger on the bus, however affectionately, would get put away.) They could not tell any other worker how to do his job; that was to cure busy-bodies. The rules, in other words, were obvious ones -- in an era when people expected mentally retarded people to hug strangers (and get into trouble for it) or dither uselessly.

If a worker broke a rule, he was fired immediately. With pyrotechnics. The terms of the firing: go home immediately; come back the next day with a note, dictated to someone but not composed by anyone else, telling why he was fired. No apology, but assurance that the person knew what it was that he couldn't do. The second firing in a year meant that a parent also had to come to the shop for the restoration. The third firing in a year was to be permanent, but that didn't happen to anyone. The rules worked.

Into this I came as the first psychologist to deal with these families, except for the school psychologists who had rejected the kids. By this time I was credentialed as a Certified Psychologist, with a state certificate for the wall of the small room that was my office. My work was nominally half time but it naturally expanded.

Neither Laura nor I knew what I was supposed to do. Actually, I did a little of everything. I didn't do much supervising in the shop, though I taught the volunteer Junior League women how to relate to the workers. I counseled when workers got into trouble or looked like they might get there, or when they wanted to talk to someone who wasn't their floor supervisor. I tested them when there were questions of why things were as they were, using a variety of clinical instruments and inventing when necessary.

Initially the main job for the workers in the Workshop was to stack paper. In this, the workers each had a wooden tray the size of a newspaper opened flat. Because many of them couldn't deal with concepts like "half full," the trays had markings around the sides: fill it up to this line, then stop. People brought their newspapers to the shop and when a tray was completed the paper was rolled and tied and sold to florists for wrapping flowers. A major concept that the workers had to learn was that of rejecting any sheet that was dirty, crumpled, or torn.

When I got there, the workshop had hired a shop supervisor, an older man who was actually retired. As we grew other foremen were hired. Gary Simon, fresh out of college, was the first new one and he quickly became the overall supervisor of the floor staff as it grew, as well as of the volunteers.

And the shop grew. It probably didn't hurt that I came from the state Vocational Rehabilitation agency, because that agency had been looking for a place to send mentally retarded people who were leaving the public schools and who needed a job. They sent to us those whom the state counselors couldn't possibly place in industry. They also sent them because I could write reports that communicated in their language and justified their spending state money on training in the workshop, and because it looked like the training we gave could lead to employment.

So gradually my work became more that of responsibility for progress of trainees, and of devising programs of evaluation and training. The state paid us because we could make a realistic vocational diagnosis, and because we could train the clients to be workers and document it.

When you work with a group who occupy your attention the way the OpShop clients did mine, you form attachments and you get indelibly imprinted with some of them.

Jim. He was one of the first crew of workers. His retardation was uneven, so much so that you might call him a savant. His big talent was in music. He *knew* that stuff. Music filled his life away from the job. He knew the names of compositions, and their composers. His interest was so intense, and his ability good enough, so that he once was allowed to conduct the Minneapolis Symphony Orchestra in a practice session. But his neurology deteriorated. His seizures became more intractable and he lost some of his skills. Finally, for medical reasons mostly, he went to the Faribault State School. Our last contact was that he had heard the theme music of an episode of "My Little Margie" and the theme obsessed him. He wanted to hear it again, and I called the TV station to find out about it. They relayed the message that the theme was composed to introduce that episode, and that it was not available - but they would tell me when the episode would air again. So I listened to the tune and memorized it; I can still play it now. I couldn't play the flute on which the sound track was played, but I had a Tonette, a little whistle-based toy with finger holes, that could substitute. Because I'm slow on the fingering I recorded it at half speed, then gave it to Jim's mother to play for him at normal speed. After he died his mother called me to thank me for giving him his music in his last months.

Karen. She came from a suburban school, where she had topped out of what they could offer. She had seizures, too. They were a source of acute embarrassment to her. But she had good sense and a willing spirit, and she was sociable once her seizures were less of a problem. Part of her improvement came from counseling where I helped her to see that, in addition to the actual seizure that she couldn't influence, she had learned some "seizure behaviors" that made the recovery from a blackout more prolonged. During the time we worked with her her seizures came under reasonable control. Anyhow, she did well on the work floor, and Gary placed her on a job with a direct mail company. (That kind of company is the outfit that takes material from an advertiser and creates the junk mail that you get.) Karen did well on the job there, too, and was outstanding in reliability. After a while she was moved up to the lead position in the line. She phoned Gary and me at home from time to time to report on how she was doing, such as when she got a raise. Meanwhile she never missed a day of work, rain or shine. She phoned us periodically after we had both left the OpShop, telling us how she was doing and that she still went to the Friday evening dances sponsored by the Minneapolis Association for Retarded Children. Still no work absences. Ten years went by; more periodic phone calls. Twenty years. She missed a day when she had an operation. Karen was now a supervisor, making good money. She still rode her bike for fun, but had a car and drove to work. My last call from Karen was about 30 years after she was placed on the job. She was pitching for two amateur softball teams. This is called success.

David. He was a big, pleasant man who had been born with 47 chromosomes instead of the standard 46 and therefore had Down's Syndrome. I had first seen David when our DVR office tested some candidates for a sheltered workshop to be founded by Easter Seal and the Kenny Institute, and in due time he was referred to the OpShop. David was quite limited intellectually and he looked the part: overweight in a soft sort of way, bullet head on a bull neck, big tongue and protruding lower lip, thick speech. But David was a true Downs Syndrome man, with a good heart (oops! bad heart physically, but great emotionally), an overwhelming sense of right and duty. He positively enjoyed working, and he would be found at the door when the first staff member came to open it. He would have worked all night if we had let him. We had to train him to accept taking breaks from the job. And David was righteous. He would come to see me and tell me that someone else was doing something wrong. I would listen and say, in a steady voice, "They shouldn't do that." And David would be satisfied; I never had to follow up on what was often his imagination. Many years later, David retired. Then, his inherently poor cardiac system failed, and he died of old age and Alzheimer's disease (common in Downs Syndrome) in his fifties. I miss David.

Actually, I miss a lot of those people. You couldn't flim-flam them about how you felt about them, because they were not confused by the words we use to lie to each other -- they perceived you directly. They had as rich a non-intellectual life as anyone, and they were in that interesting time of life when people move from childhood to adulthood. Their adulthood was not exactly like that of the rest of us, but they were adults. The general public fawned over us for "being willing to work with those people," but if I wanted to have a satisfying life I'd opt for an OpShop.

The technical side of life went on, too. In those days here was no technology for the vocational guidance of these young people. These were youth for whom the conventional educational and vocational tests could only say that they were unemployable. What was needed was a technology for discovering the potentials, the things that could be built upon to make the person employable. In the light of professional history in this field, my main contribution was that of helping to invent and systematize the techniques of what became known later as "vocational evaluation and work adjustment." Within that field my biggest contribution was related to general employability -- not the question of occupational choice, but the matter of being able to work at all.

Regular vocational aptitude tests were unrealistic for our clients. For example, a popular test of mechanical aptitude (and, in the general population, a valid one) was the matching of cut-up pieces with a completed geometric figure. Now, one of our clients might have even normal mechanical visualization with real objects, but would almost certainly be defeated by the assumption that those pictures were somehow real. An abstraction that we all take for granted would probably not be feasible for our clients. Or more simply, another test might assume that the person could read, and this would flunk our people.

Now remember, in standard industrial psychology the purpose of testing was to screen out applicants who would not be able to do the job. The industrial tester didn't worry about what happened to the people who were correctly screened out, and certainly not about people who were incorrectly screened out. There were plenty of applicants. And in the nature of history it was the industrial aptitude tests that got moved over to being vocational counseling tests. But we already knew that our people were poor test takers but not necessarily poor workers. What we needed was testing techniques and instruments that would reveal potentials and show us what could be done, not tests designed to screen out poor bets.

The obvious solution was to test our clients with real objects. Since ours was a workshop we used the objects of industry. Our best source of this was the scrap from the Minneapolis Honeywell experimental lab. There, they were always making, testing, and discarding devices. The devices were state of the art, with rivets and bolts and screws and soldered wires and both mechanical and electronic components. Some were on the cutting edge of the industry. For example, we got as scrap a half dozen aircraft autopilots. The ones we got were set up for ballistic bombing, but when the first chimpanzee went up in space, the newspaper photo showed him sitting behind an autopilot identical in appearance to the ones we got -- so one of our units went to show-and-tell at school with one of the Krantz kids. I still have it.

Honeywell also must have got back from field repair a lot of the temperature controls that stick their tubes into industrial furnace stacks, together with their remote eight-inch-square electronic control boxes. We got pallet loads of these.

All that stuff was work for our shop. The workers used common hand tools to break the objects down into salvageable parts and metals. The sales of scrap paid their wages. In addition to scrap iron there was aluminum and copper wire. One day, all the silver contact points that came from Honeywell relay switches were packed up in a barrel labeled "surplus electrical parts" to keep it safe and shipped to a refiner. It weighed over 100 pounds, at a time before the silver market crashed.

I turned those control boxes into a semi-standardized test of basic hand tool skills. The new worker was given a control box, together with screwdrivers, pliers, hammer, and diagonal cutters, and told to take it all apart. All the pieces were to be taken off, and the wires cut close to the solder joint. Then I observed the work to see what was the state of this person's mechanical skill and familiarity with tools.

By this time none of our new clients had been to the (for that time, wonderfully progressive) Home Study School. They had been at home and some had been institutionalized. In either case, they had not been entrusted to use tools. They had been told that they were going to break things if they touched them. And here I was, telling them to use tools to break something.

Many had not learned to make ballistic motions, such as swinging a hammer or tossing an item onto a scrap heap. One might grip the hammer right up by the head, and push rather than swing. That was common. Even when shown what a screwdriver was for, some would grip it right at the blade, rather than by the handle. This isn't so illogical, when you come to think of it; get your grip close to where the work is. But that's not the effective way to hold a screwdriver.

To force a ballistic motion, I'd position the box for parts too far away for them to place the parts into it. With encouragement they then had to toss the parts, and all their lives they had been told not to throw things. Could they learn to do that?

I turned the whole setting and the task into a clinical test. This idea had been discussed in psychometric literature, but it was considered to be too clinical to be practical. It isn't. I trained a couple of Junior Leaguers to do it and to record their observations, multiplying my time and institutionalizing the procedure. The instruction manual I wrote for them became a sort of local classic among rehabilitation counselors, the few other workshop professionals, and even the University.

In order to make vocational diagnoses and to design training programs I had to conceptualize "employability." When you come to think about it, and especially if you want to write professionally about it, you find that this concept is not as easy to pin down as it seems it should be. Maybe it's easier now, because of the pioneering work we did. I devised a criterion-referenced scale of basic employability that created some stir and ended up in the professional literature. Its components were rather simple minded, such as: attendance -- the person is absent from the job for any reason no more than 12 days per year, to meet the standards of industry. Isn't that simple? but it was new at that time.

From the standpoint of the state Division of Vocational Rehabilitation, which had sent the youth to us in order to have a useful vocational diagnosis made, this simplicity was made to order. We were able to tell the referring counselor, "This person has this deficiency in employability (being picked on, for example, being made the butt of co-worker jokes -- and that will get the victim fired, because the foreman won't fire his whole crew). And to make him capable of being placed on a job, you/we will have to fix that deficiency (coaching in coping techniques, reduction of stigmatizing behavior). The training program should consist of so many weeks of work here or in some other sheltered workshop." This gave the counselor some concrete things that could be done to fix the problem. I organized this sort of diagnosis into reporting forms and rating scales.

This led to my forming a sort of local club of people who were interested in formulating and testing employability, and in training clients in gaining it. There were foremen in some of the other local workshops for the physically handicapped, some of their professional administrators, rehabilitation counselors, and University Psychology staff. We'd meet and compare notes, and we'd write papers to discuss. Well, I'd write most of the papers. But everyone discussed, and the discussion was an essential sharpener of my theories.

By now, I was a little far afield from anything that could be readily given a title when the kids were asked in school, "What does your father do for a living?" I was off the edge of the normative practice of psychology, and I wasn't a counselor as such, and I didn't do industrial work. Those days were the beginning of the cloud of ambiguity that obscured the nature of my work throughout my careers. Even I couldn't say from one time to the next just what I was doing, because I was always building out from the last base of duties.

This went on for the two years that I was a student. I had planned to be titled as a clinical psychologist, but I didn't fit the profile of such candidates, and instead, I ended up with two very useful years of non-degree graduate study in rehabilitation counseling. Then I went full-time at the Opportunity Workshop. It was not much of a transition because I had been working a lot more than half time.

Meanwhile the shop was growing. A new building was constructed to house two floors of shop and instruction. We even had a cafeteria to use as a training site. Eventually the bungalow itself was demolished and a more conventional front office took its place.

We had some new staff in the shop. One of them was Fritz, another man fresh out of college. He was talented in fun, and in art. There was the time he took some silver from electrical relay contact points to a friend in the University Dental School, and made a couple of castings by the lost-wax process. One of them was a quarter-inch human hand, middle finger upraised, made into a tie tack. Another tie tack was made by casting a house fly, burning it out of the mold, and centrifuging in molten silver to duplicate the fly down to the leg hairs. I did more simple castings in the shop's pottery kiln.

The Honeywell scrap rolled through. Many of the smaller electronic components had no scrap value and plastic was not recycled in those days. We had a dumpster bin outside my office window, and I would periodically look in there and salvage interesting objects like little switches and transistors. In those days a transistor was a quarter-inch-long cylinder with three wires sticking out of one end. I took home a collection that grew into several drawers of components, that the Krantz boys could play with when they developed an interest in electronic things. We went from building magnets out of wire and nails to serious projects that they constructed.

I like to think that this had an influence on three of our kids going into electronics.

Late one afternoon I heard rummaging around in the dumpster outside my window, and there were two boys digging in the scrap. I went outside, cutting off their escape. They thought that they were in trouble. But I showed them where the really interesting stuff was and cautioned them about sharp edges and unstable mounds of junk, and they came back a couple of times. They were Sheldon and Randy Bey. We didn't know then that our paths would cross again. (Sheldon later married my daughter.)

The technology of prevocational evaluation, as we still called it, continued to develop. From several centers, of which we were not one of the most prominent, it grew into an increasingly respectable professional specialty. I had some correspondence with other developers of the technology. Prevocational evaluation was a technology for vocational diagnosis. There was not, as yet, a similar growth of explicit technology in work adjustment, the technology of correcting deficiencies in employability. (There still is not, because the movement was highjacked by psychometrists and the clinical element was suppressed.)

The director of special education for the Minneapolis Public Schools, Dr. Evelyn Deno, talked with our director, Laura Zemlin. Out of that, after some internal discussion, grew a joint project to see whether our new technology would be of use to public school students.

The school year was nearly over but we cobbled together a trial of this. Laura was the initial conceptualizer of the trial. It fell my lot, as usual, to structure and document it. Some 14 students in senior high who were at the point of dropping out were selected. (In those days, almost all mentally retarded students were gone before the end of the 11th grade.) Laura and I interviewed the parents and their students after the schools had broached the subject to them. Almost all of the families agreed to give it a try.

The students came to the workshop by bus for half of each day. The other half was spent in their home schools. We used our usual testing and training procedures, which by then had been fairly well regularized.

This went on for about six weeks. I conducted the exit interviews and probed for our staff's experiences that I had not directly observed or participated in. Then I wrote up the project, describing the students' characteristics and needs for further education.

On the strength of that, Dr. Deno wrote an application for a Federal grant to import rehabilitation technology into the public schools. The grant was funded. I wrote to Dr. Deno saying that I was of course interested in heading up the research project, but that there was a better man available, Dick Henze. Dick got the job. And I -- but I'm getting ahead of myself.

Earlier, I'd said that great and novel endeavors like the Opportunity Workshop have to be founded by zealots. More balanced people just don't defy conventional wisdom and inertia and get those things off the ground. Laura was such a zealot. And she fell into the trap that awaits zealots.

I was getting fairly prominent in the service community. Other United Way organizations were in touch with us about our technology, and I was the one they talked to, not Laura.

My office had been moved to a construction trailer behind the shop while the front office was being added to the shop. This tended to isolate me. Then came the day when the periodic meeting of colleagues took place in my trailer. We had the professional people from other workshops and the rehabilitation centers, together with a professor from the University. Our topic was, as was getting common, the techniques that we had each developed, with emphasis upon the ones I had formulated and written up. Unknowingly, I ignited a fuse.

Laura had been getting uneasy over my associations. Hadn't she been the one who taught me all I knew about mental retardation? (She had taught me a great deal. Let's be fair.) And wasn't she the one who had created and run the Opportunity Workshop whose work was being recognized?

She decided that I was giving away trade secrets, and that I was undermining her leadership. Bear in mind that the shop had grown in both size and in scope of services. We were getting in multiply handicapped clients, many of whom were not mentally retarded, or at least not mentally deficient. And she was a zealot who did not have the training and credentials to back her up as she led the shop into this expanding role. She was nervous. Actually, she imagined more than was true about me.

So one winter day she asked me to stay after work to talk to her. She and Katherine, who chaired her Board of Directors, sat down with me. With no other explanation she told me that they had concluded that it was best that I not come in to work next morning or ever. Would I please clean out my desk and go.

So I went home. Bernice said, after I told her what had happened, "Now they've done it. They won't recover from this!" In a way, she was right. This was the beginning of a time of upheaval at OpShop. After me, Laura fired just about everyone on the staff, one after the other, and the shop itself went into a reorganization in order to keep its status with the United Way and the state agencies. The Board was replaced and in a few months the Board accepted Laura's resignation. She had fallen as most zealots fall.

Similarly, Sister Anna Marie, who had founded the Christ Child School for mentally retarded children in St. Paul, saw her agency grow beyond the stage where one zealot could run all of it. She hung on until she became an embarrassment to the Diocese and had to retire, and even retirement didn't give her the ease of letting someone else take her "baby" and run with it.

On the other hand, Louse Frazer was a zealot who had been in the game long enough to achieve the foresight to hire and train her replacement, and was able to turn the school over to him when the time came for her to retire.

Laura could not make the transition to management of an agency that went beyond her scope, even though she was responsible for the growth, and she took the fall. It was unfair of life to put her in that position, because she had indeed created a whole new service system, but that's the way it usually goes. If the OpShop had not been so successful, maybe Laura would have stayed a few years longer.

I was out of a job with zero notice. I had to find another one. But within two weeks I had six job offers, and took the one I really wanted. I signed on with the project in the Minneapolis Public Schools that I had had some role in establishing. That's the next chapter, and I'm afraid that it also was a poor platform for stating plainly the answer to "What do you do for a living, Daddy?"

THE SCHOOL-REHABILITATION CENTER
MINNEAPOLIS PUBLIC SCHOOLS
1962 to 1966

In the preceding chapter, I described the pilot program that married workshop-based rehabilitation technology with public special education. And I mentioned the fact that I moved from the position of workshop psychologist to a position in the public schools.

After being fired from the OpShop I had several job offers. I had naturally kept in touch with the project that had been started in the Minneapolis Public Schools and as that was one of the offers. I took the job there.

The Project Director was Dick Henze. While I was Minneapolis District Supervisor for the State Division of Vocational Rehabilitation, Dick was one of the half dozen or so counselors who had been sent to work in my office because, I think, our state office wanted to give me a hard time. They sent me all the potential "poor prospects," whether because they were too obstreperous or (as in the case of Dick) they didn't look like much to the old guard. Little did they know. Dick was quiet, but he was well trained in educational psychology and he was an extremely able and pleasant person. I had assigned him to the troublesome school sub-office, and never regretted it.

Now he was my boss. Our relationship had always been independent of boss-employee elements, and we were simply professional colleagues. Dick's management style was oblique. I never hear him give a direct order, but he always indicated the proper direction and his leadership was never doubtful.

Above Dick in the hierarchy was Dr. Evelyn Deno, the Director of Special Education. Above her was the Superintendent. So we were well positioned.

Dr. Deno was, and still was in retirement (She's unfortunately dead now.), nationally known in special education and in other work with handicapped people. Her style was similar to Dick's. It fell her lot to write my performance reviews later, and I recall one of them that I saw (in those days, one's personnel file was not as open as it is now). My writing style, she said, was often difficult to wade through, but it was full of sound reasoning and analyses, and had good ideas. Apparently, some of my stuff was hard to understand. In retroactive defense, I fall back on the quote from Russell: in any communication, there is always a trade-off between precision and clarity. There is also a trade-off between simplicity and accuracy, between readability and substance. Son Don is one of the few exceptions. He can write interesting and simple technical prose.

Our project, selected as a national prototype, was called "Project 681." It had a formal title, the Minneapolis School-Rehabilitation Center. We were housed at the old Minneapolis Central High School, literally under the front steps. We took over what had been a janitors' storeroom and made it into an office. In addition we had the use of four classrooms: two classrooms as such, a large shop, and a home economics room. We set up simulated work stations of clerical and assembly kinds. There were classes, mostly on practical matters such as how to get and hold a job but also some in basic education.

My job was entitled Research Psychologist. Actually, there were three psychologists on staff: Dick, Ken Barklind, and I. Ken, I seem to recall, joined Project 681 later. We also later gained Gary Simon as a job placement coordinator after he too was fired from the OpShop.

With Dick, I devised protocols for educational-vocational diagnosis. Dick, who had done some follow-up research on our kind of potential caseload, had devised parent interviews and had validated them. I contributed prevocational testing techniques. Together we devised formats and techniques for gathering information from a student's school record, from structured interviews with teachers and parents, and from the student's in-Center experiences so as to make a vocational diagnosis.

Relieved for the time from direct case duties, I also did a number of research investigations. I began to establish patterns for understanding the nature of "mental retardation in the educable range," the arena in which we were working.

In Dick's follow-up data I found (actually, it was so obvious that I can't claim to have found it) a geographic pattern to the phenomenon. I made a number of other investigations to clarify the meaning of the pattern.

First of all, you have to know something about what "mental retardation' and "educable mental retardation" were.

In those days, the professional literature didn't make a clear distinction between mental retardation (the current performance of the person) and mental deficiency (a lack of brain power). So there was a great deal of pessimism about what you could do to help rehabilitate these people. Some of the professional literature, heaven help us, called them "retardates." IQ, except among the higher-level theoreticians, was considered to be something you were born with. A few studies had shown that it wasn't true that a retarded person always remained retarded but the bulk of the literature discounted these instances as missed diagnoses.

Enter our Project, situated in a public school system and dedicated to helping "educable mentally retarded youth" make the transition from school to a job. Educable mentally retarded youth had IQs in the range of about 70 to 85, together with a demonstrated inability to profit from standard classroom education. Because they were so close to normal the idea was that they could profit from school, but the school system for them had to be different. So, as they began to fail in school and had been found to test low, they had been placed in special classrooms where the pace and expectation had been lower. They had not done well academically and most of them dropped out of school before they were 17 or 18 years old.

Our Project was charged with using imported rehabilitation technology as well as educational techniques to both make their last years in school meaningful and help them become employed. It was for the purpose of doing this that I undertook several lines of research.

The geographic pattern of the students' residences was striking, so I mapped it. The only good index we had of the city's sociology was the rate of juvenile delinquency, so I use that as the index. I soon found that only 27% of the city's total youth lived in the core census tracts that were in the upper two quintiles of delinquency, but that 65% of our student lived there. Remember, this was a couple of years before the War on Poverty started, and nearly five years before that "war" produced good data. My conclusion was that our kids were not more delinquent than the average, but that their neighbors were. That said something about the subculture (the word was not yet politically incorrect, and I could use its meaning of "a distinct grouping within the city's culture").

I checked other populations. The patients at the Faribault State Hospital, who were too retarded for what were then the community services, were random on the general population; only 25% of them came from that city core where 27% of the city's youth lived. The population of the Owatonna State School, which took mostly delinquent youth who could be tested into the retarded range, was geographically distributed just like our students. 65% had come from that central area of social deterioration.

I was later able to get other indexes of social deterioration. In Minneapolis, a city with the classic ring pattern of development, the central city had the highest delinquency, renter occupancy, welfare use, bad plumbing, person-per-room rates. And that's where our educable mentally retarded people came from.

Now I have to apologize to the reader. Unless I explain what I found in my research, you really wouldn't have an idea of what I did - not exactly for a living, but while I was earning a living. This research, like most of the significant things I've done in my life, was self-assigned and self-directed, and those who hired me in most of my jobs didn't hire me to do that. But most of them used and valued my findings and insights.

In any case, my career makes sense only if you take into account the things I did that were important to me, and that I think had some influence upon my field. You won't find much of a bibliography of my works of that era, because by the time the findings were accepted someone else was doing the writing. Sometimes I was credited. Most of the time, my work just went into the mill.

In what I now want to say about my work with mental retardation, you have to take a historical perspective. The term isn't much used now, I think because it makes people uncomfortable. No one ought to be retarded, so we won't say that it exists. This kind of ostrich verbalism is one reason I'm glad to be retired. Historically, in those days, there was such a thing and it was important to educators.

Now to get technical. There are, it turned out, two kinds of mental retardation. There is one kind, caused by some single event like being born with 47 instead of 46 chromosomes, which knocks you clear off the normal curve. Most of the people who have one of those catastrophic events are not only seriously mentally retarded, they are mentally retarded because they are mentally deficient. That is, they lack brain functional capacity. They have the fairly rare clinical types: Down's Syndrome, phenyketonuria, brain malformations and perinatal brain injuries, etc. They comprise only about ½% or 1% of the population, and they are the minority of the people who are mentally retarded.

But most people who are mentally retarded are not mentally deficient. Bear in mind that an individual's performance capacity at any one time is the result of the impacts of a multitude of factors.

(Now you have to pick up the picture of a normal curve, the curve of how a phenomenon is distributed when it's multi-causal. If you chart some human trait, like height, you'll find a normal curve, with most people bunched up in the middle and fewer and fewer as you go out to the extremes. The shape of the curve of people's distribution is a very particular one, and one that has a very distinct mathematical shape. Repeat: this normal curve is what you get if you tally up any multi-caused phenomenon, like height and IQ.

(As with the curve for IQ, the curve of height has a bump on the bottom, caused by the rare instances where a single catastrophic event throws the person right off the curve -- genes for dwarfism, for example. They are, like the clinical cases of mental retardation, not normal curve results, and we will set them aside from our present discussion.)

The non-clinical cases of mental retardation are multi-causal. When the implications of this are understood, your first reaction will be, "But are they mentally retarded then?" Yes they are; but the reason that they're mentally retarded is not that they are mentally deficient. They are functioning as mentally retarded; that is to say, they have low IQs at that time and, against the life criteria they face at that time, they aren't making it. That's all mental retardation is. It is a different and separate question as to *why* they are mentally retarded, and what you can do about it.

At school age, the important life criterion is academic performance. If you don't do reasonably well at academic studies, you aren't making it. If you are doing spectacularly poorly, and are not obviously doing poorly because you aren't trying or because you are disturbed, you'll be tested and you are likely to have a low IQ. This proves nothing about the amount of smarts you were born with, though it may in some cases. But are you mentally retarded? you bet you are. Are you mentally deficient? maybe not, or at least not enough to explain why you function so poorly. This will cause some purists to tear their hair and yell, "Missed diagnosis!" and in fact, our findings were at first dismissed on those grounds.

But this distinction between mental retardation and mental deficiency gives reason for hope. If the factors at work on a person, and the factors that were at work in his formative years, are multiple, then there is a good chance that they won't stay constant. In fact, they don't. And the odds are good that, as the factors change and new factors come into play, the new constellation won't be as damaging as the extreme constellation that was at work before.

Furthermore, our optimism was strengthened by our knowing that, if we didn't just keep slugging away at the same special education that hadn't worked for these people, we might get different results.

Finally, although our sponsors didn't realize it at first, nor did we, we had on our side not only the phenomenon of regression toward the mean (a person who is far out, on the next deal of the cards isn't likely to be so far out), but also the change that comes from the person functioning against a very different criterion. These people were poor performers in the classroom. Very well, we didn't use much of a classroom approach. More to the point, we could train them to meet a non-school criterion, the job.

Enough people in important positions realized this in 1962 to enable our project to be born and live out its life. The masses of people in psychology and special education did not realize it. We met with a lot of skepticism at first. More precisely, we were recognized for our techniques and results but not for our insights.

To shorten the story, I did some intensive population studies on our clientele, and our project reported what they were like and what they needed.

The population I studied most intensely was the 1962-63 ninth grade of educable mentally retarded students, 138 in all. In the course of doing that I entered onto McBee cards the data, together with my judgment of what influence certain clinically-judged factors had on their academic potential. I also entered my prediction of their employment outcome. Then I sealed my pack of cards and removed it from the schools, though I did give a duplicate set of data to the school office. The usual data remained in the student record: IQs (there were usually several), age at entry into special education, whether the family was intact or broken, etc. No one who subsequently dealt with the students ever say my judgments and predictions, so that they would not be influenced by them.

(Fifteen years later, I gave my pack of cards to Guynell Reid, a doctoral student at the University. She at first was given only the name, birthdate, and 1963 address. After she had interviewed 85 of them, she opened the pack of cards and checked the now-known outcome against the raw data, my judgments, and my predictions. The raw data, such as IQ, didn't predict outcome. My predictions were significant at the .0009 level with actual employment. That is, there are only 9 chances in 10,000 that I was guessing about their employment potential. As far as I know, I'm the only vocational clinician whose predictive power has been calibrated and validated in this way.)

(I had started the Ninth Grade Study by having Ken Barklind independently make the same clinical judgments as I was making, but after the first dozen it was clear that we were nearly identical in our ratings. So I went on alone. I think that the validation of my predictions can be applied to the validation of Ken as a clinician also, even though his judgments were not recorded.)

After the first year, Ken and I were re-titled as Case Managers. As far as we could find out we were the first people in the country to have that title and those duties, although it is rumored that someone in New Jersey and/or Missouri was before us. A case manager is the person who is responsible for mobilizing all the resources that are needed by a person in order to meet a need -- in our case, the need to successfully finish school and get into employment. The most easily identified function of the case manager is that of counseling, but beyond that, there is simply nothing that is *not* his duty in the cause of meeting the person's needs. The concept was new in the schools, though it is implied in rehabilitation counseling. We were not carrying out a set of services, but we were doing and scrounging and mobilizing whatever was needed.

We called upon the student's internal resources, our vocational diagnostic powers, the our Center's staff and services, the family cooperation, the school where the student came from or continued, community agencies such as the State Division of Vocational Rehabilitation, and employers. We bent rules when necessary. Those were great days.

We extended the definition of counseling. If counseling is a process of helping the person to: understand his circumstances, his abilities, and his limitations; understand the options and choose among them; settle upon a goal and a course of action and enter into implementing it -- then we were carrying out counseling in the round. It was no longer a matter that was to be carried out over a desk, it used the whole situation as well as words. This may be old hat now, but in the early 1960s it was novel.

And we talked about what we were doing. Because we were designated as a national prototype project later in the five years of the existence of Project 681, we had visitors from other states and systems. Before that, though, we continued in our professional associations and contacts, and we talked about what we were doing and finding. The word got out.

Eventually, bureaucracy caught up with us. The State Department of Education noticed that they were paying part of the salaries of some people who were not credentialed in education. I, for example, had had exactly one quarter of one course in education, and none in special education. And here we were, getting paid state aid as special educators. So Dr. Deno got creative. I was already a Certified Psychologist, and she wrangled me a Life Certificate as School Psychologist II. Now I was legal. Similar arrangements were made for the others.

We had great and creative times. We were breaking new ground, and we were striking fire off each other every day. We were excited, even the phlegmatic ones among us. One Saturday morning, in the grip of a killer migraine, I composed a 13-page poem of my insights on mental retardation. (See, in my archives, *Hiawatha's Fishing*.) On the job we all did new things routinely, and gave each other warming approval. Once in a while we alarmed the conventional school people, but by and large they appreciated our taking some problems off their hands.

Dick and Dr. Deno were involved with the planning of the metropolitan-wide association of 45 school districts, the Metropolitan Educational Research and Development Council. Out of that evolved a plan to clone our operation to serve a more severely retarded population, pooling metro-wide resources and student bases to deal with a proportionately small but numerically significant problem. In 1965 was created the Cooperative School-Rehabilitation Center at Glen Lake.

Our project had run its life. Its grant-supported time was up. We had a ton of working papers and it was time to write a final report. We all worked on it. But as usual, I did most of the writing, accounting for all but one chapter. It was called *Mentally Retarded Students: their School-Rehabilitation Needs,* and authored by Deno, Henze, Krantz, and Barklind. I cite all that, because I can't tell you to read my copy. My copy was copied and loaned so many times that it got lost some years later, while we were still getting requests for reprints. None of us have copies anymore. I have an archive of many of working papers, though.

At the end of the project two things happened. One was that most of our Project 681 staff moved over to the new Cooperative School-Rehabilitation Center. Dick became the Director there, also.

The other thing that happened was that our operation was institutionalized by the Minneapolis Public Schools as its own center, located in the old Washington School near downtown Minneapolis. We continued much of what we had been doing.

I was made the Center's Director. Most of us knew at the time that this was a mistake, but there weren't many choices. We would have to grow someone to become Director and do it right. I am not an adequate administrator, but we had to do what we could.

Since we were now an integral part of the school system, we had to refine our relationship with the other schools and systematize it. We did that pretty successfully. Dr. Deno backed us and gave us both entrée and advice, and we came off well enough so that the Center became a long-living part of the school system.

One of my achievements was the creation of a maximally-efficient system for using our Center as a school resource. We were more expensive per student-day than a conventional school, so we had to ensure that we were called upon when, and only when, we were actually needed. So I devised the "cascade system" for student flow. I built two less-costly levels of service that we could extend out to the schools before they physically sent a student to us together with the rules for invoking the levels in order. I called it a cascade because its diagram looks for all the world like a set of cascaded transistors. The term "cascade" became understood by some others to mean "the whole array of services," but that only annoyed me without impairing the effectiveness of the system.

Except. There was a parallel person in the schools' special education department who wouldn't play by the rules, and who had the authority to bypass the system. He and I got into a shouting match and thereafter avoided each other. Good man, but as stubborn as I am, and without the ego strength that permits compromise. And he was on my turf.

Anyhow, the cascade system worked this way. When a high school called us with a problem of schooling a mentally retarded youth, our first package was a one-person consultation. In the past the routine would have been to refer the student to our Center. Now we first went out to them instead. If that solved the problem, it was finished at low cost. If, and only if, no satisfactory solution came about, we invoked the second level. Our second level was a more intensive consultation, involving a systematic pickup of records and interviews, plus if necessary a new psycho-vocational examination of the student. If that solved the problem it was finished at medium cost, and still without disrupting the student's school career. If it did not solve the problem, and only if it didn't, then we could invoke the third level, a period of time in our Center.

The math of this cascade of services is iron-clad. It is the most efficient way to apply resources, if they can be organized into levels of intensity and cost. I may not be a good administrator, but I'm a good system designer. And, like Akhnaten and Don Dabelstein, I was the first to have this insight and to also have the power to set up the system. Only the one person tried to short-circuit it, and all that he accomplished was to cost the school system a little bit more.

We initially didn't have the resources for the second level, apart from myself. So I devised a set of operations to do the assembly of detailed information that would be needed in the second level. There was a protocol for interviewing the people involved with the student and for abstracting records, and indicators for when a fully professional psychologist would be called upon.

As part of the same issue we created three positions for counselor aides. The idea had been talked about but it had not been carried out in a controlled manner. We decided to fill the positions by taking the first three applicants "off the street," with no screening by preconceived criteria beyond a BA degree of any kind. My conviction was that we could train any reasonably intelligent person, basing that conviction upon my experiences with Junior League women at the OpShop.

We got three people, all of whom were adequate and two of whom were so good that they nearly ruined the experiment. They hardly represented random selections from the population. One was a social worker with some experience. Another was a minister's wife with abundant energy and enthusiasm, intuitive grasp of human affairs, and a willingness to absorb technical matters. (That was Grace Engnell.) She stayed on for some years, in fact, and became essentially a professional counselor. So the experiment was a success, and we could vouch for the sense of using counselor aides, but we couldn't vouch for anyone else having the degree of success that we had.

In any case the Center operated fairly well, even without a skilled administrator. I learned that, in a school building, the principal (I was sort of that) is subordinate to the janitor.

But I was restless. This wasn't my cup of tea, and I had no more good ideas in that spot.

I had of course kept in close touch with our clone, the Cooperative School-Rehabilitation Center in Glen Lake. Dick and others knew that I was restless, and after a year as a Center Director I took a job as Assistant Director for Research and Development at CSRC.

COOPERATIVE SCHOOL REHAB CENTER
1966 to 1974

The Cooperative School Rehabilitation Center (CSRC) had been somewhat cloned from the Minneapolis project, and its cadre had come from there. It was located in Minnetonka, in one of the buildings of the former Glen Lake Sanitarium. I had done some work at Glen Lake when it served tuberculosis patients when I was a rehabilitation counselor.

Dick Henze, the Director of the Minneapolis center, became the Director of CSRC. Gary Simon, with whom I had worked at the OpShop and in Minneapolis, filled the role of CSRC school Principal. I had been left in Minneapolis with those staff members who were tenured in that city's school system, plus those added for that year. Most of my familiar co-workers were already at CSRC.

My job at CSRC was that of an Assistant Director, officially in charge of research and program development. Finally I had a title that went with the kind of job I was eminently suited for. I was not in the administrative line but was positioned where I could work with whatever and whomever was needed to evaluate and improve our program. Finally I had a job title that would have made sense -- but by then our kids were no longer in elementary school, and they couldn't go back and tell the classes that "My Dad is an Assistant Director in a special school."

Our clientele was "less able mentally retarded adolescents." What that came down to was shaped by the federal law that mandated that all students, including those seriously handicapped, had to get an appropriate public education. The 45 school districts in the Twin Cities Metropolitan Area had previously joined in an association, the Twin Cities Educational Research Council, to foster expansion and improvement of public education. The member districts were (in those 1960s) faced with a mandate that they were not prepared to fulfill. Up to that time schools were only required to serve "educable" children, which meant that they served mentally retarded kids only down to IQs in the upper range of retardation. They had neither the skilled staff nor the other resources to take the "trainable" mentally retarded kids.

(If you want to know the practical and theoretical meaning of those matters, you'll have to look up my report of the Ninth Grade Study and its working papers, particularly those dealing with mental retardation itself. They were written in the mid-1960s, before the subject was well explored elsewhere and before it became politically impossible to write plainly. They're in my file box of archived papers, if it still exists when you read this.)

Anyhow, the kids who were sent to CSRC by their home districts were those who were too retarded to fit into the services to the educable retarded, and who were yet mobile and could talk. They were bussed to CSRC from their home districts each day. They were all at the high school age level. The role of CSRC was to work out an appropriate educational program for them, provide it, and get them from completion of school to establishment in a job. CSRC was begun on need and hope, and had to work out both an appropriate educational program and a transition to adulthood for young adults who had previously not been expected to do anything useful in their lives. We began by importing methods from the Minneapolis Schools project, and we went on from there. I had been somewhat involved from the beginning, even though I remained employed in Minneapolis for that first year. (The final report of the federally-funded project that was CSRC is in my archive box also, because I wrote the report.)

114

Some of my work at CSRC was that of an "in-house consultant" to the staff, part was the digging out of information for research and program evaluation.

Another, more prominent role, was that of "outside man at the skonk works" (Dick Henze was the "inside man," in addition to his Director duties.) I led tours for dignitaries and professional visitors, and I did a lot of the outside speaking. I was the most visible liaison to professional organizations such as the Minnesota and National Rehabilitation Association and the local (and to some extent, national and even international) Council on Exceptional Children and the Association for Retarded Citizens.

One of my duties was to automate the program management information. Dick Henze arranged for us to get a teletype terminal and to link into the primitive mainframe computer that was operated by the Metropolitan Educational Computing Consortium, an inter-district school service. Since I was about the only CSRC staff member who wasn't tied to a schedule, and since I was thought of as a technical person, I was put in charge.

The modern reader will have to visualize the teletype. It was a small console with a keyboard and a printer, and with a mechanism on the side that could punch and read a paper tape. The printer slugged along, noisily, at three characters per second, spinning and jolting a little cylinder of type against the paper. It was hooked up by phone to the mainframe computer in Roseville. We were blessed with two assets that made my job possible: a secretary who was somewhat familiar with the FORTRAN computer language (working from punched cards) and my son Don, who at age 15 was pretty good at programming in languages like BASIC as well as at the ones-and-zeros of machine language. With their help, I mastered the job.

I don't want to make this sound as though my main job was to run the "computer" system. It was a necessary sideline, but a sideline. My main job was research and program development and program evaluation. Plus, as usual, writing the results.

The duty was a learning opportunity for me. I learned simple BASIC programming, because we were linked into the regional educational computing system on a time-share basis. This basis had been devised to enable schools to give students access to computer programming, which even in the late 1960s was visible as a coming field. What it meant for us was that we could design our own programs, which we would have had to do anyway since our school operated so differently from conventional schools.

We shifted from the student-scheduling program that we had been setting up on punched cards. Son Don helped to build the necessary programs and maintain them. By then we had about 150 students, with as many as one third of them changing their class schedules in a given week. We had to keep teachers informed of who would be arriving at each hour, so we fell into the routine of changing schedules at staff conferences on Thursday to be effective the next Monday. My job was to see to it that each teacher and Case Manager received, by Friday afternoon, the lists for Monday. The secretary or I would feed the changes into the computer and set the teletype to slugging out the paper. The print-out could stretch the length of the hall, and took three noisy hours to print.

The time came when we wanted the computer to search for class openings, so that we could optimize the class loads. I didn't know how to do that. I went to the headquarters of the computing consortium from which we rented time shares, and asked for consultation.

They were surprised at what we were doing, looked it over, and said that their computer couldn't do what we wanted. I went back and called in Don. He sat down at the console and typed for a few minutes. "Now it can," he said. And it could. He never said what he did to that computer in Roseville, and I never told the consortium, but my bet is that he reached into some part of the system that wasn't supposed to be available and altered the computer's capability.

Our first four years at CSRC were the sort of thing that people really enjoy in their jobs. We did what we wanted to do and what we sincerely thought we should do, with minimum effort wasted on meeting regulatory requirements. As far as that goes, a major part of my job was to relieve the front-line staff of some of their documenting and justifying work and to so enable them to get on with educating. In my program development work I was the one who often came up with ways to work more efficiently, without trying to micro-manage. Dick Henze, as was his forte, took care of negotiating program enablement with bodies like the federal funders and regional school districts, singly and in their association. We made a good team.

CSRC used a variety of program methods and curricula. We had an active physical education program. We had an academic program that was directed toward adult-readiness. It taught the basics of sign "reading" (recognition, mostly) and it taught math as the process of making change. Our teachers were an exceptionally creative bunch, several of whom later went on to make names for themselves in special education (two district or regional special education directors, one state director in Montana). We ran a Montessori program that used professional-exchange teachers from India and Holland. We used other professional-exchange teachers in other parts of the program, from an assortment of countries. Dick Henze made those innovations. We used aides creatively, ignoring formal qualifications in favor of real resourcefulness and ability (several of those aides went on to full educational qualification in later years). Again it was Dick Henze who recruited and selected these people. Dick had an exceptional talent for selecting good people for jobs that were often ground-breaking in nature, and for managing them so as to bring out their full potential.

We were relieved of some of the normal regulatory restrictions on the grounds that were an official research and development project (R&D) with substantial federal funding, and that we were trying to do what the regular educational system could not do with its normal resources and technologies. Both Dick and I worked on maintaining this freedom, he in official channels and I with voluntary organizations and through legislative involvement and monitoring.

While all this was going on at CSRC, I was active in professional organizations, sometimes going to national and international conferences to present our work. Also, my consulting work on my own time was significant, mostly in psychological work-ups for the Opportunity Workshop and the Disability Determination program of Social Security. This consulting work, however, was never heavy enough to take my attention away from CSRC.

As Assistant Director for research, I often collaborated with the CSRC instructors and other staff, mostly in program evaluation. For instance, CSRC wanted to see whether the Montessori program was contributing to the competence of the students, and whether certain of the techniques we were using in other classes were effective. My job was to design the research and its data-gathering instruments, and to tabulate and write up the results in concert with the instructors involved. Some of the pertinent papers are in my archive file.

We used Case Managers at CSRC in roles similar to what they had played in the Project 681 in Minneapolis. Each Case Manager was assigned a caseload of students and was responsible for the programming of those students at CSRC, for parent and student counseling, and for liaison with the student's home school district. We started with few, three I think, and increased to maybe six plus a supervisor of case management, Dr. Ann Meissner. Ann was a practical and capable woman my age, an intellectual Earth Mother and an effective line manager. For one year, while she was on (educational?) leave, I took over the line job of supervising the Case Managers as well as doing my other work, and I was nowhere as effective as Ann but did contrive to keep the program going adequately.

We had characters in the student body, and characters on the staff. One of our prime character students was Peter. He was an active and impulsive adolescent, always exploring. He was fascinated with the elevator that we had in our headquarters building, the old Children's Building of the Sanatorium. One day I came down to the office to find Peter in the office, looking distracted. He loved to mop floors because he could wear rubber knee boots, and now he was holding his knee above a boot with a flap loose over the toes. What had happened to his foot, I asked him. "Drop a rock on it." "Show me the rock, Peter." So he limped over to the outside door and pointed to a five-pound rock we used as a doorstop. "Peter, you didn't drop that rock on your foot. Show me where it happened." And Peter led me to the elevator.

I wasn't too surprised. Peter had once been caught standing between the inner and outer doors of the elevator (the outer swinging door was solid, the inner one was one of those collapsing grids), having closed both doors and reached in to push the button, and had ridden down one floor without getting killed. This time, he had gone into the elevator and closed both doors. Then he had stuck his foot out through the grid door and played Russian Roulette with the floors, pulling his foot back at the last moment as the floors passed a couple of inches away from the rising floor of the elevator. Well, he had lost at one floor, and the guillotine had caught his foot.

I took off his boot and found that the stocking was similarly torn, but his foot was only mildly bruised and not bleeding. Nothing was broken. His parents, who knew Peter, were not upset at CSRC.

Peter is also the person who contrived to – you see, our building had window wells in the basement, and one day a shrew had fallen into the well beside the wood shop. The shop teacher had placed the shrew in a birdcage to show the students, and had turned his back. Peter opened the cage, took out the shrew with his bare hands, and held it while he wiggled its nose with a finger. A shrew is the closest animal analogue to a buzz saw, and it had immediately bitten Peter's fingertip. We had to keep the shrew until everyone was sure that it wasn't rabid.

Peter later moved with his family to North Dakota, in the grain country. Finally he had a kind of elevator that couldn't harm him.

Peter wasn't the only student character we had, just the most memorable one. Incidents short of disaster were always happening, and disaster never happened. It wasn't that our lives were charmed, but rather that we took reasonable precautions, offering as open an environment as possible without being irresponsible. That kind of stance is not possible now, in our less trustfull society. By the same token, success such as ours in no longer possible, either.

All of us on the staff were characters too, I suppose. Dick Henze wasn't afraid to hire characters if they were creative. One of our most visual characters was Elaine Hartzman, a Case Manager. Elaine had been born with athetoid cerebral palsy, a condition that distorts motor impulses without harming the intellect. Elaine is very smart and resourceful. She later went into private practice as a psychologist specializing in marital counseling and women's issues. She is most memorable for her saying (in a setting, CSRC, where you could say such things and not be misunderstood), "Hire the handicapped, they're fun to watch." She had been educated in an elementary special education program with "those nice polio kids," who we knew from our rehabilitation experience to be tough competition -- on the surface -- for a kid who had trouble talking plainly. So Elaine is a scrapper, but with a sunny disposition and a wide sense of humor as well as professional skill. She held her own, and better, in our mix of able people.

Our bond as a working group was extraordinary. Since none of us had been hired to play out a conventional job role, we had to work closely and to depend upon each other. Years later, we still keep an interest in each other and I get invited to such things as farewell parties for those who are retiring from the jobs they progressed into. Quite a few are still doing the jobs they created at CSRC and took with them elsewhere.

We used the Sanatorium, which still contained a few people with TB but was mainly a state-operated nursing home, as our training environment. For instance, our students were trained in the San cafeteria. Gary Simon, who was the Assistant Principle and also the leader of our job-preparation program, invented a system of remote instruction for the bussing students in the cafeteria. He used FM receivers worn by the students and a transmitter to give instruction throughout the room. It is important to give reinforcement and instruction immediately with this population, more than with a non-retarded clientele. For marginally verbal people, it doesn't do much good to explain what should have been done when the work setting is not immediately before the student. The radio transmission allowed the instructor to be "in the ear" of the student without following around in the room. Gary and I wrote up this successful instructional experiment, and it was adopted in other settings. For that matter, I'll bet it is still being used in some places.

CSRC was 'way out in the Minnetonka countryside, being in a former TB Sanatorium. The idea when such sanatoria were built was to get those TB patients out of town, only partly because country fresh air was thought to be good for them. In relation to CSRC, that meant that all the students, who came from the whole western metropolitan area, had to learn bus transportation, including the use of public busses when a transition to work was in order. We had an active bus training program going.

Most of the students left CSRC to go into some kind of employment. Gary and the other transitional staff located job sites, sold the idea to employers, saw to it that the students made the trip safely, and followed through with enough on-the-job training in basic employability that the job could be permanent. In those days you never saw a retarded person in a competitive job until we and a few other schools nationally constructed the job transition program. Twenty years later, I could still sometimes see our former students still on the same or similar jobs where Gary and his crew placed them.

After a couple of years it became evident that the students on the east side of the metropolitan area were not going to be able to use CSRC because it was located 'way over on the west side. That meant that a new "CSRC" would have to be created on the east side. Since I had done the research that established the need for and feasibility of an east metro "CSRC," I was given the task of setting up the new center.

My work had put me in touch with the people on the east side who would have to create such a center. I spent parts of the next few months exploring and negotiating with them.

I quickly learned that my earlier analysis of the politics of the metro area was correct. In the west metro, centered on Minneapolis, "deals" are brokered formally, and are sealed with a written agreement -- which participants then start to search for loop-holes. In the east metro, centered on St. Paul, the deal is worked out informally and sealed with a verbal agreement, usually in a bar, between power brokers who may not hold official positions, but it then holds firm but flexible. West metro is Scandinavian-German; east metro is Irish.

We got a center going, and it ran for a while under the same aegis as did ours, namely the interdistrict council. It was even called East CSRC. It reflected the changes that had taken place in special education since CSRC was formed, as did we. But an administrative change was coming.

After four years CSRC was given a permanent, non-R&D home. A new special purpose school district had been formed, the Hennepin County Vocational-Technical Schools. It was multi-district in geographic coverage but was a legal school district within the state's vocational-technical system. When it became operational CSRC became its first operating unit, later to be joined by vocational school campuses in Eden Prairie and Plymouth. The two campuses are now the North and South Hennepin Technical Colleges.

We became responsible to a formal school district, and Dick Henze became a Director within the vocational-technical system. I kept my position and my duties.

Gradually, the district came to make use of my abilities. At first they wanted me to move into the district office in Plymouth, but I resisted. There was a certain amount of stiff-legged stalking around each other between CSRC and the district, they wanting us to shape up and be like other schools and we wanting to be free to do what we had found to be effective with this population that they had no experience with. We ended up with our freedom, hedged about with the respectability of the district. Dick Henze's diplomacy paid off, and he became visible to the district as a valuable man in their responsibility for the education of handicapped youth.

Other roles were added under our umbrella. The regional program for deaf students and for blind students were brought into CSRC, housed both at the San and at the district office. The district-wide program (all of west metro, on contract with schools not in Hennepin County) for elementary "less able retarded" pupils, with the actual programs scattered in the constituent districts, became part of our job.

Our continued ability to operate CSRC in the way it had to be, regardless of our administration under vocational education, was in part due to the support we had among the school districts, the parents, and such lobby groups as the Association for Retarded Citizens. Part of my job was to mobilize those supports as needed, without antagonizing the district office.

Our Superintendent was an energetic man who had no background in special education, who was fairly flexible, but who had his own reputation and status to watch over. My visibility in the community made him nervous. Once, I was present at a district administrative meeting where he was reporting on the status of the state legislative actions that impacted vocational education. He was making a point to the School Board members present, and turned to me out the blue and said, "Krantz is active in the halls of the Capital," and asked me to confirm what he had said. I of course did, though I wasn't in touch with that particular item. My support seemed to reassure him, and things went more smoothly. I think that he was afraid I'd do something in the community that would upset his apple cart, but naturally I wouldn't do anything like that.

I did have quite an impact on the emerging mandate for vocational education, nationally, to serve students "with special needs." At that time the federal mandate was being worked out. Definitions of special need were fluid. I had met with the state administrator who was in charge of developments in Minnesota, and after the meeting I sent her my usual 13-page letter confirming the substance of our discussion. Some two years later, I lost my copy of the letter, and asked her to make a copy and send it back to me. She sent the original. Its upper left corner was a lacework where the staples had been pulled and re-stapled as it had been copied and sent around the country. I can't point to any one way in which that letter affected developments, but I did hear indirectly of its being the subject of discussion in various conferences. It was things like that that made my Superintendent nervous.

He did ask me to undertake one special job for the district that didn't involve CSRC. I was asked to find out what the vocational campuses were doing to meet the new mandates to serve students with special needs (handicapped and socially disadvantaged). I put together a three-person research team, hiring two aides. We designed and implemented a survey that is in the archive box. It had some statewide impact, and its reasonably favorable tone helped to take the edge off the district's nervousness about me and the rest of CSRC.

But the survey was the last of my assignments. I had been working in special education for 12 years without any educational credentials except a license as School

Psychologist II. I was clearly not doing what those people normally do, and I'd had only one quarter's course in education. The state Department of Education wrote to our district and said that they could no longer provide reimbursement to the district for the employment of people like me (there were a couple of others), unless we went and got training in education. We had a year to comply.

I was ready to move on, anyway. So I turned in my badge and went back to school. With the help of a professor in Educational Administration, Dr. Richard Weatherman, with whom I had done a number of consulting jobs, I enrolled in the doctoral program. He was to be my advisor, and I knew of his reputation as one who moved his students through.

TEACHING ASSISTANT II
1974 to 1976

The date was 1974. I was 50 years old. I had been told by the state credentialing authority that I had to get a degree in education in order for my position to be funded in the schools. So I went back to school as a student at the University. I never did return to the public schools as an employee.

Again, Wife Bernice became a mainstay of the family finances. As a Teaching Assistant again I had an income of sorts as well. The kids were all grown and out of the nest. Later we changed roles and I supported the family while Bernice got her BA at Metropolitan State University.

I was enrolled in the doctoral program in Educational Administration. Never mind the fact that I had determined that I was not management material; the coursework was in administration rather than management. I figured that I could use the Ph D in just about any job. Besides, I had grown tired of being introduced, when I spoke, as "Dr. Krantz," and then having to explain that no, I didn't have any such degree.

I had worked with my major advisor, Dick Weatherman, on a few consulting jobs, often for the Educational Management Corporation of Edina. So we knew each other well, and he knew what to expect of me, and he handled the politics of the Department for me.

One of my fellow students was a man with whom I had also worked on various consulting jobs over the years, Warren Bock.

As Teaching Assistants or Junior Scientists, I forget which, Warren and I went to work with Dick on a federally funded project that they had secured just before I got there. This was to make a scale to measure overall competence in living of mentally retarded people. This scale became the Minnesota Developmental Programming System, the MDPS. It came out in finished form in my second year in the Ed Ad department, and contained 18 scales in domains such as Self Care, each with 20 nearly ordinal statements of behavioral competence in increasing order of difficulty.

Partly because I'm a systematizer and partly because I had built other behavioral scales I became the theoretician and editor of the effort. I also traveled to West Virginia to examine that University's library of behavioral scales, and wrote them up in a summary that had some currency locally and even nationally -- informally, of course. it wasn't published. Although we all three worked to develop the scales, with the other two contributing at least as much as I did, it fell to my lot to be the word merchant, writing texts and manuals as well as the internal memos that structured our work technically. It was an exciting time, with each of us sharpening the others to the task.

While we were doing that minor but interesting consulting jobs came our joint way, and Dick and Warren and I became out-of-town experts in a number of things. You'll find most of that in the chapter on Consulting.

Working -- and being a graduate student -- in a University department is a revealing experience in its own right. Like most graduate assistants I had a sort of office, or at least a desk, and thereby a fixed residence within the building. The Department of Educational Administration was small, with maybe a dozen regular faculty, and all of us in a fairly small building, so I got to socialize with my professors. They were a mixed bag. One professor was the man who had been the liaison for the Twin Cities Metro Educational Services, the official sponsor of CSRC, and I had known him for some eight years. He was the intellectual powerhouse of the department. Another was a specialist in school law who was then the Chairman of the department. He had his mistress as the departmental secretary and we never heard that his wife minded. One of the two computer-and-systems specialists was the department's statistical instructor, and the other was a younger man who was skilled but not a member of the inner circle. Both of them were quite helpful to me. Then there was my major advisor, Dick Weatherman. In him I was fortunate to have an advisor who believed in moving his students through and getting them degreed. With his help I did all my course work for the doctorate in one year, and wound up my thesis in another year. When you consider that I'd had only one course in education before starting, and that most doctorates take about seven years, some satisfaction is reasonable.

My employment as Teaching Assistant in the second year was mostly focused upon the competencies needed by the people who were heading up the then-new "special needs" programs in vocational education in the nation's post-secondary vocational schools. The work became the basis for my doctoral thesis, where it may be consulted. It was pretty pedestrian work, involving getting information from practitioners. It necessarily didn't determine what competencies were actually needed, but only what the practitioners thought that they needed.

(For a couple of years after the thesis became available for citation, I was treated as the expert in the programming for student with special needs in vocational education. After that, I dropped from sight in the vocational education field. This kind of expert is short-lived.)

While working on the behavior scale I had a great and rare opportunity. I was sent to a summer seminar in Snowmass, Colorado. That turned out to be the meeting of the nation's experts in program evaluation:

Scriven, Ionacone, and the rest. I found myself one of only about 25 people who took part in the brainstorming that gave birth to the national professional association of program evaluators. All but one of the big names of the discipline were there, and I found myself accepted as one of the boys for that week and, in correspondence, afterward. What I learned there stood me in good stead in subsequent consulting work.

Another satisfaction at the Snowmass conference was that I got into a semantic argument with Mike Scriven, who was arguably one of the three most powerful philosophers in the field, and I won. And then Scriven proved that that was what he had meant all along. Nobody out-argues Mike Scriven.

The work as Teaching Assistant ended with my educational career. My PhD was granted in June of 1976, and my next job was on the other (Minneapolis) campus of the University.

CONSULTANT IN HUMAN SERVICES
Various years

This section is not strictly chronological with respect to the other chapters, but it fits here as well or as ill as it would elsewhere.

In any profession there is opportunity for extra work as a consultant while doing regular work. There is also the option of doing consulting work as the sole job, but I didn't get to that until much later, and then it wasn't really full time.

A dry recitation of the various consulting jobs, each given only two lines in my 1986 vita, takes over two pages. That's 37 different jobs up to 1984, after which I quit keeping that kind of record. In some of these consultations I was one of a small team. In others I was the solitary consultant. A few of the more interesting ones will be recounted here.

While I worked for the Opportunity Workshop, after having been a vocational rehabilitation counselor and supervisor, and being a state-Certified Psychologist, I did some off-hours work for the Social Security Disability Determination unit of the state Division of Vocational Rehabilitation. The state had to determine whether an applicant for disability benefits was truly vocationally disabled, and I was one of the relatively few psychologists in the state who was experienced in disability and vocational matters.

In most cases I'd get a request to examine an applicant for benefits. I'd be given only the barest facts about the person and would work up my own vocational diagnosis. In simple cases it would be a matter of determining whether the person was mentally retarded enough to be unemployable (in those days -- things are different now).

I generally went to the home of the applicant and interviewed family members as well as giving clinical tests of intelligence and personality. My reports must have been effective, because I wasn't called to testify at any hearings and I understood that the benefits had been granted.

This went on in an episodic way for a few years, only a few per year. Then I got a half dozen referrals in the space of three months and detected a pattern. Remember, I was never told what to look for, but until then the people's problems had been varied and random.

But these all had a history of brain damage from a stroke or from an accident, and all had damage on the non-dominant hemisphere. All had retained their speech (this is usual in those cases. The right side of the brain is non-dominant in right-handed people, and a right-side stroke usually affects the left half of the body and does not cause an obvious speech difficulty). All had been seen by neurologists who reported that the person was fully recovered from the neurological damage. And none appeared to have obvious problems but in all cases the vocational rehabilitation counselor believed that the person was unemployable. So here were people who were given clean bills of health by neurologists but who couldn't work. Were they disabled? The answer couldn't be pinned down.

Once I learned that they were non-dominant hemisphere cases, I had a clue. It wasn't widely known then (it's now known to all psychologists), but damage to the non-dominant hemisphere causes subtle but serious problems.

One example, I'll call him Charlie. He was 48 years old and had worked all his life. I went to see him and noticed that he had his jacket hanging on a peg on one side of the arch between the kitchen and dining room.

Why was that? Well, he said, he hung the jacket there to pad the arch because he was always bumping into the side of it there when he went into the kitchen. And that would be the left side of the arch, though he of course didn't think of that. So I gave him an individual intelligence test, and he came out in the normal range but with some subtle hints that he wasn't grasping certain tasks. For example, when asked to multiply two two-digit numbers, he could come up with a ten-digit answer and see nothing wrong.

Then I had him draw a person, and he drew the right side (head in profile facing right, right arm, and right leg). I asked him, "Didn't you forget something?" and he said, "Oh, yeah." And he put a hat on the man.

I asked him what he did with his time. He said he went for walks. "Any problems?" Yes, after he'd gone a couple of blocks he didn't know where he was. How did he find his way back? He asked people the direction of his address. How did he know that he was home? Well, the sidewalk was a different color. I went outside and he was right; there was a new section of sidewalk in front of his house.

By now the diagnosis was clear. This man was disabled. His spoken language was not damaged but the deeper structures of language were bollixed up. His judgment was impaired. And he had left-side agnosia, being unable to reliably attend to objects on the left side, though his vision was perfect. He could not safely operate machinery or drive a car (he could see, but get no meaning from, a car on his left). I made my report and he got his benefits.

The other five were in the same boat. It turned out that the agency was using me to see whether a psychologist could find and effectively describe the disability in these cases. Other psychologists were not finding this kind of problem because they had not known about the phenomenon (as I said, they do now). I knew about it because I'd been in touch with the Kenny Institute research on the subject, and because I always looked behind the IQ to see how the person's mind worked.

I got mad about being used as a guinea pig and quit working for Social Security. Maybe I shouldn't have, but they didn't financially make it worth my time anyway.

Other consulting, this time in 1969. Each state was mandated to produce a statewide rehabilitation plan in order to qualify for federal funding. Minnesota hired a man with great credentials (until they were re-examined after the project blew up) to write it and endless commission meetings and public hearings were held. I took some part in the meetings as a professional rehabilitation worker who wasn't working for the state. And the project ground to a non-productive halt with the deadline approaching. It turned out that the man whom the state had hired was charming but incompetent and he couldn't write. I was engaged by the State Planning Agency as a consultant to "edit" the State Plan. As it turned out, I had to hold a couple of meetings to force decisions and to write the whole Minnesota State Plan for Vocational Rehabilitation myself. Actually, I typed the thing personally. You'll find me listed as the editor.

I did a number of other small consulting projects over the years, but one that was ongoing after I was fired from the Opportunity Workshop, and after the lapse of three or four years, was to do the psychological work for the Op Shop itself.

This was straightforward examination to determine the fact of mental retardation (for the purpose of state eligibility) and of determining the handicaps and abilities the person would have on the work floor.

The results were not always straightforward because mental retardation is not some unitary thing. A mentally retarded person has as much intra-personal variation as anyone else, and the IQ no more describes him than it describes, say, you. In addition, there are some commonly occurring special problems that require that the examiner be alert to their possibility.

For example, it is not uncommon for a mentally retarded person to have better visual-motor decoding than encoding. What this means is that the person can see his mistakes better than he can avoid them. He may do a task, know that it didn't come out right, but not be able to fix it. Conversely, he may lack the perception of mistakes but not be correspondingly prone to make them. These things have important implications for both task assignment and supervisory style in a workshop. It would be my job to clarify this.

I worked as a consultant to the Op Shop for some years, off and on, as the need arose.

A University professor, Dick Weatherman, was in touch with our work at CSRC because his department, Educational Administration, had taken a major part in forming CSRC. He was also in touch with some of my off-job consulting work. When the time came to shut down the Owatonna State School, Dick and some others mobilized a team that included me to examine the situation and make recommendations about the 150 or so youth who were resident there. We examined the cases of each student -- I wrote the data-extracting protocols and managed the data gatherers -- and found out what we were dealing with.

The Owatonna State School was nominally for "educable mentally retarded" youth. What it actually was, was a place to send young people who at a crisis in their lives could be tested into the mentally retarded range, but who couldn't be tolerated by their communities. They had been there an average of three years, and in those three years their IQs had increased an average of ten points. (Not because it was a good school, but because of the statistical phenomenon of regression toward the mean -- I'll explain that sometime, or you can look up one of my papers on the subject.)

For nearly half of the kids, community resources had developed well enough in the preceding years for them to return to their home communities. Many of them were not bright, but they certainly weren't mentally deficient. They would require vigilance because they tended to be holy terrors. During their stays in Owatonna most had been involved in fire-setting or assault. The median number of car thefts *while they were supposedly in a semi-secure facility* was one per person. One of them had gone out to a local heavy-equipment yard and played bumper car with a big bulldozer.

Many of the girls had been removed from their home communities because of incest. The boys tended to be simply acting out their maladjustments. Another large proportion did need an institutional school, but not the one at Owatonna. They were the ones who had to be taught how to survive in a community to their own benefit and to the peace of the neighborhood.

A very few were indeed mentally retarded in the standard sense, and they transferred to other state schools. That was just before the great push for deinstitutionalization.

A new kind of facility had to be built for the majority kinds of kids who had ended up in Owatonna, and we specified just how to operate it. The state took our advice and built the Minnesota Learning Center at Brainerd and put the Owatonna school principal, Warren Bock, in charge of it. That took some couple of years to accomplish, of course. Meanwhile, Owatonna itself was tightened up to carry them through.

The report that established the structure of the Minnesota Learning Center in Brainerd had me as consultant to the private firm of Educational Management Services, Inc. I did a small number of other consultations for them, such as program evaluation of the "Role of the Michigan State Schools for the Blind and Deaf" in 1977.

We all got a kick out of playing advisor to the state, and having most of what we recommended implemented. I personally gained a lot of professional networking that paid off in other consulting work, most of it minor. My archive (if it survives) will give the details.

The Minnesota Department of Public Welfare engaged me in 1975 to make a study of the mentally retarded people who were resident in nursing homes around the state. I drew upon available records and made a mail survey to fill in specific data. The report fed into the plans then being formulated for deinstitutionalization and more appropriate placements. Technically, nursing homes were the wrong places to place mentally retarded people, but one of my findings was that in many cases the mentally retarded person was the adult child of an elderly nursing home resident and this was a way to keep families together.

One of my favorite consulting projects was the work for the West Metro special education coalition in 1975, with state funding, to run a three-day conference on the procedures required by the new federal and state regulations on special education.

For this I prepared a series of systems analyses, embodied in charts and workbooks, and group exercises to trace out the main requirements of the regulations. I won't go into details on this, because it was a very complex matter, but will claim that the basic flow charts were adopted by the state education department with little modification. My archives contain the work on that.

While I was a student in Educational Administration, I contracted with the quasi-state Minnesota Commission on Fluctuating School Enrollments to examine the factors in teacher mobility. This was a piece of cake, taking only a few dozen hours, and it didn't hurt my University career.

There were a number of one-shot or one-day consulting jobs that I took, usually in the company of one or two other Minnesotans. For instance, I was a paid "Resource" to the West Virginia College of Graduate Studies in 1976, in a three-day conference to develop guidelines for special needs in vocational education. Like some other gigs this was a great opportunity to meet and hobnob with national experts, most of whom were far better known than I and all of whom were fascinating. Another such one-shot "imported expert" conference was for the 1977 workshop on special needs in vocational education hosted by the Northcentral Ohio Special Education Service Center.

The 1979 Conference on Independent Living Rehabilitation in Tulsa, Oklahoma was similar. By then I was in my short-lived fame as an expert in that field. And I was still in vogue in the Vocational Special Needs Articulation Symposium hosted by the Minnesota Research and Development Center for Vocational Education in 1980. There, I tried to clarify the definition of "articulation" as that of agencies working in synchrony -- a lost cause, I found.

As I look at my older vita document, I find a number of consulting jobs that made no enduring trace on my memory, though I presume that they were adequate at the time because I got paid.

But some jobs are still vivid. The sessions in New York stand out.

In 1979 and 1980 I was part of a 3-man team from Minnesota who were called in to New York to help the city determine what to do with the people in Single Room Occupancy housing (SROs) in the upper West Side, west of Park Avenue near 98th Street. There, for many years, old apartment buildings had been cut up into single room housing operated something like residential hotels. The housing was cheap, and the tenants were "strange." At each SRO there was a caged "registration desk" inside the front door and this constituted almost the entire security.

In the late 1970s it became profitable for developers to buy up these SROs and convert them into high priced condominiums. The first few such events caused no disruption, but as the process proceeded, the city began to have problems. Where would these tenants go? Who would provide housing in their price range, and where would they be accepted? So, since the city could not come to grips with this themselves (due to mostly political pressures and turf wars -- isn't it always that?), they called in Minnesota experts.

Warren Bock, whom we had first encountered as school principal at the Owatonna State School and who had become the Director of the Minnesota Learning Center, was already working with New York on one of its institutions for the mentally retarded, a notorious snake pit that had to be closed down. So he was asked to bring in a team to help with the SRO problem. Warren, Dick Johnson, and I made up the team. Our job was to define the SRO tenant population and their needs so that New York could make reasonable provision for them in different housing.

We traveled to New York several times in the course of this, first looking over the territory and then working out how to study the population and their needs. The area was so tough, just two blocks off Park Avenue, that we were warned not to go into the buildings alone and never to go there at night.

My job was to devise the data structure and forms for picking up the information about the residents and to analyze the data. I had a Selectric typewriter and I got the type ball that would allow me to type up data-gathering forms, with the data combs and boxes that would let the surveyors (New York employees) record the data. This was in pre-computer days, you may note, and very few professional people were able to construct these forms. We met with the data gatherers to tell them how to fill out the forms. We met in the MacDonald shop on the Avenue, with bag ladies and their shopping cart "homes" on the sidewalk and with a few derelicts rambling in and out. When the forms were completed,I subcontracted with a local man to punch the data onto cards and run them through the University's mainframe computer. Then I wrote the description of those strange people who lived in the SROs and turned it in. We didn't ever find out what happened to our work, and it probably was dissipated in the toils of the New York bureaucracy.

But while we were working on that, a crisis arose. The State of New York moved to shut down the Men's Shelter in the Bowery for exceeding its licensed capacity two-fold, the Shelter sued the county for non-support, and the city Welfare agency got caught in the middle. None of the agencies could define the problem because none of the other agencies would let them for fear of bias. It was an impasse. The City and State got together by phone and decided to call in those Minnesota experts.

Warren, who knew New York politics from his work with their State Welfare Department, handled the arrangements. We all three went to the Men's Shelter to look at it.

The Shelter was, naturally, in the Bowery district. That is not a good neighborhood. The Shelter was in a tall building. Its day room looked just like the day room of a state mental hospital in the pre-reform days of the 1950s: some men slumped at tables, out of it; a young man striding back and forth across the front of the room, shouting his lecture against his enemies; another young man in the rear of the room, going through ritual motions; another man talking non-stop against a wall. Clearly, these men were not just suffering from poverty.

We looked at the dormitory room. In this large square hall beds were ranked with space to walk between them. At night, we were told, two armed guards patrolled constantly and even then there were casualties. The toilets off the room were only half operative. It was a constant battle to clean out the broken bottles that men had tried to dispose of there. In a wire cage to one side was the psychiatrist's office, with its heavy mesh ceiling holding up assorted thrown bottles and other objects that had ended up there. The psychiatrist was one of those unusual men who couldn't meet the social demands of private practice, but who was one of the few who could tolerate working there and who was apparently as good at his trade as one could be in those circumstances.

In the office of the Shelter Director the head man was on the phone, his voice sounding normal but his face crying and his free hand slamming down on the desk as he pleaded for funding from someone. Then he finished, and talked with us warmly and calmly but pointing out the organizational and financial problems under which he labored. He introduced us to the vocational counselor, another man who might be a misfit elsewhere but who was actually having some success in job placement of the residents.

Then the time came to force decisions. Warren set up a meeting with the three agencies involved, and I set up the process by which the decisions could be reached in this den of enemies. I used a modified nominal group technique, with pre-prepared forms for reaching decisions.

In the morning we met with our SRO workers in the MacDonald restaurant. In the afternoon we met on the 104th floor of the World Trade Center with the agency representatives -- who had never been in the same room together before, and who each had an agenda that conflicted with the others. I chaired the meeting, and walked them through what needed to be decided before we could proceed.

It turned out that, though no one would say so openly, there was one item of information that no one wanted us to find out: how many of these Shelter men had been discharged recently from a state hospital for the mentally ill? If we had found that out and reported it, the State would be in trouble for discharging the men before they were ready, the county would be in trouble for not furnishing follow-up services, and the Shelter would be in trouble for having residents that they were not licensed to serve. So we returned home and I undertook to devise the data pick-up and its analysis.

To get the information about the men we set up forced interviews. Our gatekeeper was stationed at the entry to the mess hall, and only after giving an interview would the man get his meal ticket. We got cooperation to the extent that the men were able. I did the data analysis and wrote the report, in which it was clear that most of the men in the Shelter were mentally ill and were from the New York area. Again, we didn't find out much about what happened as the result of the report, but we did have the satisfaction of getting those enemies agencies into the same room for the first time, and getting a decent three hours' work out of them.

Three scenes remain in my mind about that New York episode. One is a cold drizzle from the sea, and walking south of Times Square in the evening and seeing the bag ladies settling into their cardboard boxes for the night, tucked as inconspicuously as possible into various nooks. Another is the drift of men, worse off than those in the Shelter, near Rockefeller Center. And the third is our own adventure, trying to leave the Shelter as the winter dark descended and finding that no cab would come into the Bowery area. So we took the subway, an adventure in itself in those days and in that area.

Other consulting jobs were derived from a small computer program that I had worked up in 1970 or so while at CSRC. This was an "if-then" little program in BASIC language, running on the time-share educational computer off in Roseville. It was a simulation of the actions and decisions that governed the movement of a handicapped person in the vocational services that were available then. It was designed to teach the most effective use of those resources: vocational diagnosis, general education, basic employability training, training in a particular vocation, daytime (unpaid) activity occupation, sheltered employment, and competitive employment. It was all reduced to a one-page flow chart, but it was original in that no one had apparently made a systems analysis of the services before. Professional colleagues tended to either dismiss it as trivial or to acclaim it as powerful insight. Later, I reformatted it into a booklet form, with notched pages to allow simulated movement of a client through the service system. I called it *Simulated Case Flow*.

Anyhow, this led to my being asked to come to various places and demonstrate the Case Flow. In 1977, I was asked to come and install it on the computer at Auburn University and to orient their rehabilitation students to its use. In 1979 I used the booklet form in a course I taught at the University of Minnesota to special education teachers. It was not a hit.

It was unfortunate,from my viewpoint that public agencies didn't adopt or adapt this approach of systems analysis. A major reason for agencies to be "irrational" is that no one agency had broad enough responsibility to be motivated toward the effective operation of the total system. It was enough for them to run their corner of it.

However, a "pup" of that system analysis did find its way into a broader context. I had become involved in the field of Developmental Disabilities planning, and ended up as the volunteer-board head of the Twin Cities Metro Developmental Disabilities Council. Over a year's planning effort, and under my chairmanship, we worked out the entire complex of services (vocational, residential, educational, even transportation) to people with developmental disabilities. We laid out all the possible services as an interrelated system, with the possible actions and the decision points and criteria identified. Our publication could have served as the blueprint for a rational and effective total system of services and to some extent, it did serve that purpose. However, this time the problem was that even professional people don't often have the grasp and motivation to make actual their often-voiced desire to "work together."

Meanwhile, I did a number of small jobs where I was called in to either moderate and facilitate planning, or to do the research that would enable planning.

The Plan of Services to Students with Special Needs in Vocational Education, 1971, was done for the state vocational education agency. There, I was mostly facilitator and editor. In the 1977 project of idealizing the Special Needs program of the Suburban Hennepin Vocational Schools I drew upon my previous work in that organization and came back as consultant to formulate the plan, get it ratified, and edit it. For the Plan for Senior High Special Education in the Minneapolis Public

Schools I chaired a series of meetings that used data, gathered from surveys that I designed, to develop the plan, and I then wrote the document.

A larger project was the one where I was called to Tucson, AZ in 1978-79. This took several visits and planning sessions, together with data analysis and proposal writing. The inter-district Pima County Special Education Cooperative covered a large territory in southern Arizona, and they needed to make systematic sense of their operations in the light of the detailed requirements that came with the then-new Federal laws on special education. I worked with the staff there and drew upon my skill in systems description to make the manual and forms they would need to meet the regulatory requirements. As far as I learned, the plan was implemented. (Consultants are not usually kept informed about what happens to their work after they leave.)

Some of my consulting jobs arose out of my work on behavior scales, particularly out of my work on the Minnesota Developmental Behavior System of scales. I had worked with Warren Bock on other jobs, and he was the one who carried the future of the MDPS when the Federal project that developed it ran out. He parlayed it into use in several states -- but, as a prophet is not without honor except in his own country, the MDPS was not adopted by Minnesota itself except as Warren and I were able to weasel it in when we worked for the state.

Anyhow, as Warren worked with other states that did adopt the MDPS or its derivatives, he would call me in to do the research, to conceptualize the systems needed, and to relate the MDPS data to management information systems. Some of these, such as with Illinois, were extensive. There I ended up writing the manuals.

In the North Dakota MDPS adaptation I did two things. One was to design and moderate the decision process in which the MDPS scores were set into criteria for placement of mentally retarded people into various levels of residential facilities. I again did the writing. A while later North Dakota decided that they needed a higher level addition to the MDPS Vocational Behaviors Scale, and Warren gave me the job on a Friday. The scale was to be delivered on Monday. It was, and field testing led it its adoption without further modification. That episode illustrates what can be done if you have a store of ideas and items available for use on short order.

A couple of years later I phoned North Dakota to find out how things had gone, expecting that they would have carried out my recommendations for further refining and validating the placement and vocational scaling criteria. They told me that they had simply used the placement criteria in several hundred cases now, and there were no mis-placements! That is, of course, improbable, but who am I to complain?

I did a few self-contained jobs for the state of Minnesota. One was the survey and recommendations regarding the residents of the Minnesota Soldiers' Home, done for the Department of Administration in 1980. The Department had priced out what it would cost them to do the data structure and analysis using their own staff, and found that I could do it for half that cost, pay a subcontractor, and make a profit.

That last one, with the work I'd been doing with Warren Bock and some other small jobs for the Minnesota Department of Public Welfare led partly to my taking a full-time position with the Welfare department, as described elsewhere.

With Dick Weatherman and Dick Johnson I did a short series of weekend trips to St. Louis. That part of Missouri, Region 9, was about to miss a deadline for planning on which federal funding was contingent. It was a mare's nest. There were several dozen school districts in St. Louis County, and St. Louis was not in the county of its name. The agencies were all at cross purposes and in chronic conflict. Skipping the details: we got it done. It's both easier and harder to do than it may appear. As was our practice, I did the writing.

I did a few small management studies for social agencies, such as residences for handicapped people, daytime activity programs, and sheltered workshops. I quit keeping track of my consulting jobs and don't have any noteworthy memories about them after I retired from my state job. Most of them were editing, writing, and "show up and be the expert" jobs, many of them for Warren Bock.

RESEARCH SCIENTIST AT THE UNIVERSITY
1976 to 1980

Back to the point in the chronology where I had finished my work on the doctorate and my work as a teaching assistant in Educational Administration.

Incidental to this, I applied for and was granted by the state the license to be a school superintendent. I took that license, and licenses in vocational education and special education administration, just because I could. I had no intention of ever being a school superintendent, and I would be a terrible school superintendent, and of course I let the licenses lapse when they expired.

With my Ph D in hand and no other job readily available, I accepted a position as Junior Scientist in the Special Education section of the University's Department of Education. The head of that department was Bob Bruininks, whom I had known in other settings and even as a neighbor in the 16th Avenue area of Minneapolis. (Some 30 years later, Bob became the President of the University of Minnesota.) The offer was prompt and the pay and fringe benefits were adequate.

What I was to do was pretty flexible. The Special Education unit was administering a number of grant-funded projects, and my main work was with the one on deinstitutionalization of mentally retarded people.

Deinstitutionalization, that big mouthful, stood for the social movement in which handicapped people, mostly mentally retarded and mentally ill, were to be moved from institutions into community settings that were to be "least restrictive" consistent with the person's abilities. This measured statement was retained even as zealots made it doctrinaire and insisted that there was no role at all for large institutions to play. Fortunately, my work did not bring me into conflict with the zealots who had taken this doctrine to its ultimate -- and, to me, its unwarranted -- conclusion that would outlaw any setting that served more than six people. That extreme would prevent the assembly of resources that are needed to serve the most severely handicapped people, those who require life support and who have no discernible interaction with the environment. As I say, I was fortunate not to have to deal with those zealots.

Life on the University campus is characterized by two things besides the obvious. One is that life is relaxed unless you put in your own motivation. The other is that there is no "there" there; no one is in charge of things and there is no real hierarchy of responsibility. Universities by design are collegial, and the result is that no one can be held accountable for such things as coordination or even discharge of duty. Well, I can be self-motivated, and the lack of supervisory authority never bothered me.

I did a lot of little things that used my skills in refining concepts and clarifying, and in writing and sometimes in speaking. There were a half dozen of us in the unit who were all loosely attached to the range of research and similar things that were funded by the diverse grants garnered by the professorial staff. There was a lot of interaction among us and with the faculty as we worked. My work products therefore were merged with those of many others, and were published under the names of the employing faculty mostly.

The sub-project within deinstitutionalization that fell to my lot was the investigation and analysis and reporting of the mentally retarded people in the state institutions nation-wide. I established contacts with all of them and devised the data- gathering tools that would let us know what the caseloads were doing. Then I would annually analyze the data and write it up in publications that were largely tabular. There is a series of these publications bearing my name as senior author. None of them is terribly thrilling to read, but they became the reference points for those who were concerned with that aspect of the deinstitutionalization movement. My being listed as senior author was unexpected; usually the faculty member gets all the credit. My name was used partly because I was already established in the literature, but also because Bob Bruininks is a fair man and a consequently respected manager. (He soon became the Academic Dean of the University.) One or more copies of these publications will be found in my archive box.

The approximately four years at the University, on the Minneapolis campus, were uneventful. Once I was asked to teach a quarter of a special education course that dealt with non-school resources as well as life-preparatory secondary special education. I thought that it went OK, but it was not well received by some students (others made a point of how useful it was). I think that I expected a broader outlook than was held by students who just wanted to get the course out of the way, and I worked them harder than they were accustomed to. The difficulty of senior and graduate coursework had dropped quite a bit since I was in their shoes. As a general rule, those students who liked my instruction were already in the field and saw the need for it. The others were still students by life-stage.

The University interlude in my career was comfortable but I could see that it would lead nowhere and would always be sort of like being let out to pasture. It was time to move on.

Warren Bock by now was the Assistant Director of the State Department of Public Welfare's Mental Retardation Division. He had been offering me positions over there. Then came the legislative "gift" of three new positions in his division to facilitate the creation of community resources for mentally retarded people. I was encouraged to apply, and this resulted in my leaving the University.

For some two years after leaving, publications continued to turn up with my name listed among the authors. As far as I could see I had only participated in formulating the works on which the publications were based, but I had not done any "authoring" of them. Finally, I asked the unit not to put my name on the publications. It was a good run while it lasted.

COMMUNITY DEVELOPMENT SPECIALIST
1980 to 1985

When the jobs as Community Development Specialist opened in the State Department of Public Welfare I was one of several applicants. There was no written exam, just a review of records and an oral interview. One of the interviewers was a former fellow teaching assistant who had gone on to employment in Hennepin County Welfare. I scored well with the others but very poorly with her. She had a different conception of case management than I and was looking for a set of doctrinaire answers. In particular she was looking for answers that fitted a particular structure of case management, and I didn't give them. I was passed only because of my overwhelming paper qualifications and the interest of fellow professionals.

I became a state civil servant again. There are a lot of advantages to such a position, not the least of which is the set of good fringe benefits and pension. In my case there was the additional advantage of working under the supervision of two men who were quite familiar with my work. Warren Bock has been mentioned. His boss was Ardo Wrobel, with whom I had been in professional contact for over a decade. Another advantage was that I wanted to do what they wanted to have done. It was a good fit.

As Community Development Specialists, our job was to see to it that the communities around the state built up the resources that mentally retarded people need in order to leave or avoid placement in institutions. Personally, I don't think that those who lobbied for the creation of those positions were very smart. In the first place the state is not a good agent for innovation and is better suited by structure and practice to *impede* innovation than to promote it. In the second place, no one has a real handle on the forces that enable the building of community resources. Social and political movements can facilitate it, but no one can centrally direct it. Well, we tried in our various ways. The most effective one, as far as I could see, was the way in which one of our number, Mary (in her spare time she was a boxer!), pushed her way into case meetings and similar settings to promote a sound set of case planning actions. The others of us did things in individually different ways.

My approach was two-pronged. One was to provide the management information that would motivate action (that was what I was hired by Bock and Wrobel to do). The other was to supervise and structure the work of a small group of regional facilitators whom the state hired to implement the innovations that our unit and others were promoting.

The information system fell into what I usually do best, which is to conceptualize service systems in such a way as to visualize the way they are intended to work -- not as a set of procedures but as a set of goal-managed actions. For this you need a systems analysis that includes actions, results and information, and a way to get the information to decision makers.

The state, as I mentioned earlier, is not innovation-minded. It had a central computing agency with an allegiance to mainframe computers and centralized data management. The era of the personal computer was just dawning and they wanted none of this irresponsible, decentralized, uncontrolled computing by individuals. So we bootlegged.

Warren had an Apple II computer that he owned personally. He told me to take it home and learn how to use it. It had a database management program, a simple but effective flat file base. I took the machine home and had the usual learning experiences. For example, I had built over half the data base when lightning struck a power line somewhere. The screen blanked out and there was nothing in non-volatile memory. That teaches you to save your work frequently, not to mention to avoid computing in a thunderstorm without a surge protector.

We were responsible for overseeing the community placements of mentally retarded people and for keeping track of the institutional situation. This was made to order for a simple database. The trick was to structure the data helpfully and efficiently and to get the data to enter into the base.

The first was easier than the second. We had to build up the channels of data reporting, which fortunately we were in position to do. We required all the community facilities that were licensed by our agency to report periodically on the forms that we designed. I handled the technical end, and Warren and Ardo and I handled the political end. Soon, which is to say in a bit over a year in the state environment, we were reporting to the counties just where they stood in terms of placement and movement of caseloads. I adjusted the reporting forms that we sent out to meet the needs that were claimed. The system worked, and for a beginning where data were not available before, it worked well.

The central computing people fumed but it wasn't their machine and they were not in charge of our division.

Then the legislature passed a law restricting the expansion of intermediate care facilities (ICFs) just at the time when we were trying to expand one kind: the community residences for mentally retarded people. By virtue of their licensing and funding, such residences were ICFs. The legislature had acted to hold down the cost of nursing homes, a different kind of ICF, but there we were. Now we had to work under two conflicting mandates.

For a year or more things were in some confusion. We never did get the permission to exempt community residences for retarded people, most of which now served only six residents each, from the general ICF restrictions. To complicate matters there were a number of large residences that were holdovers from the early days of community placement and they were in the best financial and management position to expand. Current policies were against such large residences and we had to wrestle with those policies.

In my last couple of years in state employmentI was put in charge of making the determination of whether to grant waivers to the limits on ICF expansion. The database became our secret weapon in carrying this out. On the other hand I was the one who had to document and defend our refusals of expansion requests before the hearings that were called for by frustrated service providers. It is never fun to be legally deposed on the subject of refusing to let facilities do what they clearly ought to be encouraged to do. This was the least comfortable part of my being a bureaucrat. But I turned out to be a good one, and this troubled me.

There were more pleasant aspects to the job. We were often able to help public agencies do their work well and with benefit to their clients. It is also satisfying to create a set of tasks (comprising for me the management information system) and see the product perform properly.

It was during this time that I decided to personally enter the era of personal computing. I bought the first of the portable computers, the Osborne. It ran in the now-obsolete CPM operating system, it weighed 26 pounds and had a 4-inch screen, it had one meg of RAM, and you had to use two 5.75 floppy disks to boot it up and to run programs. But it was as good at word processing and database management (given the state of those arts) as is the also-obsolete DOS (still sort of available as the Command Line of modern computers). I used it on some consulting jobs, adding an external monitor when possible and printing out the results on a modified Brother daisy-wheel typewriter. I kept it around until 1998, partly for sentimental reasons and partly because it was the only machine that could translate a CPM disk into DOS format.

The time came when we could add regional development specialists to the Division staff. I, as the now recognized leader in case management, was put in charge of them.

Because they had to serve outstate, away from the office, I picked up the concept of the "virtual office" from the Scientific American and worked it into a system. Now common, the portable office was unknown in 1983. I even got a name in some quarters for inventing the concept of the virtual office, but as you see I was only a developer and systematizer.

The state of technical art had improved. Now you could get a self-contained portable computer with a real 10-inch screen and with acoustic and direct modems and a dot-matrix printer built in. It was the Actrix, and it was a cube with a handle, about 12 inches each way and weighing 35 pounds. But there was nothing that came close to it for portability and completeness. So I requisitioned six of them.

The requisition was routed through the computer division of the Department, and the lords of mainframe blew their stacks. This was rank palace coup, and they sat on the requisition after calling me in and demanding, but not understanding, my explanation of why I should want such machines. If any computing was going to be done, *they* would do it.

Could they take data from the field, over the phone lines, do the computing, and send back results in the format requested? Oh yes, they were thinking of making their machines accessible by phone (but certainly not in real time) and submitting the data by batch and in order of priority, and they could send back information that could be hand-tallied in the field. How long would it take? Well, a couple of years before they had the ability, and then a week or two to process and return the information.

I went back and re-wrote the requisition. Then I hand-carried it past the data managers and got the signatures. The machines were delivered (though with a different word processor than was requested, because the purchasing department got a deal) and we set them up. We installed a public-domain word processor that worked like the one we had wanted, and a shareware database manager.

The data people found out, and demanded to know how we had slipped the requisition past them. It was too late now; we had the hardware. I had to go to the usual stormy meetings to clear it up, but we were in business.

By then I had learned that I could retire on pension in a few months. The "Rule of 85" had gone into effect, by which a state employee could retire on pension if his age and years of public service totaled up to 85.

We hired a young man fresh out of the St. Paul Technical School, Jeff Hove, to be the computer expert. Warren and I had had some very favorable experiences with him when he came over, as a student on work-study, to be a short-term apprentice. As things turned out our faith in Jeff was abundantly rewarded in subsequent jobs, when he took a position with Warren in the private sector a couple of years later. The man is a genius who became at least as good a systems analyst as I, probably better in the present work environment.

Jeff was fully able from the technical standpoint though he was not able to replace me in the more general roles. So I left with a management system running and with the beginning of virtual offices, at the point in time when the personal computer was coming into its own. After I left both systems were changed in response to changing needs and in the light of the basic conservatism of the state. Both were just a bit ahead of their time, and I was no longer in charge of them. *Sic transit* whatever.

Now I was retired. In my waning State days, Bernice and I had begun our wandering with a trip around the world with the excuse of a professional paper to be read at a conference in New Delhi.

RETIREMENT I, BRIEFLY
1985 to 1991

After leaving the State Department of Public Welfare I maximized my pensions by buying back the years of retirement that I had earned in 1959-1957. I had had to take my retirement funds at that time, because they would not have been vested until I'd had ten years of state employment. It cost a significant amount of cash to buy back those retirement rights, but the math worked out so that I got it back in increased pension within a half dozen years.

Pensions were still not enough to live on. Bernice was employed by the Minneapolis Public Schools as a special education aide and this would have enabled us to get by. However, both the opportunity and the inclination put me back into the private consulting field. As Ulysses is made to say by Tennyson,
"How dull it is to pause, to make an end,
    to rust unburnish'd, not to shine in use!
As though to breathe were life! Life piled on life
    were all too little, and of one to me
Little enough remains ..."

So I took a job here and there. You'll find some of them, out of chronological order, in the chapter on Consulting.

Then an opening showed, and like a "retired" fire horse, I charged out to answer the bell.

SYSTEMS DIRECTOR, LIFEASE, INC.
The Development and Marketing
of the Program EASE
1991 to 1995 or so

I was sure that I had one good arrow left in my quiver. And I did. Then, at full draw, the bowstring broke.

All the while I was consulting after leaving steady employment with the State I had the uneasy feeling that there was at least one more big thing that I could do, one more project into which I could pour my creativity and energy.

In November of 1988 I was in the office of Emeritus, Inc. Warren Bock called to me from his open office door, "Hey, come in here, I want to show you this!" So in I went.

Warren had two people in his office whom I didn't know: Margaret Christenson and Adam Lindquist. Margaret had come to Warren to see if her Home Environment Checklist could be computerized, and Warren wanted my opinion before he went into it. Actually, the meeting wasn't entirely adventitious, because Warren had said to Margaret, "If Gordy says it can be computerized, we'll do it." I looked over her many-page checklist, gave a top-of-the-head opinion, and said I'd go home and study the issue.

The checklist was a clinical format for an Occupational Therapist to use in examining the home of an elderly person in the light of the occupant's condition. When a problem was found the checklist offered a short statement of what products could be gotten or what could be done to correct the problem. It was far too long to be useful most OTs, and it wasn't systematized completely. But it was good material.

So I wrote a long memo of what I thought, and reviewed our discussion. My basic conclusion was that the checklist could be computerized readily enough but that its internal logic would have to be reworked according to a scheme that I charted, and its concepts would have to be regularized. Briefly, the home occupant (an elderly person, whom we called "the client.") would have to be assessed for limitations, then the home would have to be assessed *using the same concepts* to compare ability with environmental demand and to allow the computer to identify problems. Logically, the lack of an ability is not a problem unless the environment requires the exercise of that ability. Each problem would then have to have a logical link to the computer's database of solutions. I charted out the basic logic of a workable program (a chart which, not incidentally, became the framework of the actual program that was developed).

Then I mostly forgot about it. I was always throwing out conceptual schemes; they cost nothing, and they're fun.

A year or more later Margaret called to ask if I was interested in helping to develop the program, which at that time did not have a name. (To save paper, let me here give you the name we finally decided upon, though we didn't actually choose it until 1990 or so: EASE. The name stands for Environmental Adaptations Serving the Elderly, but that's not important.) If I were interested, would I have dinner with her husband and her to discuss it?

We met at a nice restaurant. Her husband Carl was an outstanding colo-rectal surgeon, and he wanted to know if Warren was a reliable person to work with. I told him what I knew: Warren is a sort of risky entrepreneur who plays the part; but that I trusted him completely myself and that he had never let me down. Warren is a lot more moral than he talks. Also, that he regarded me as "his boy," and that I let that fancy go as unimportant. As a direct opinion, I told them that Warren was the best "shop" I knew of to undertake the computerization of EASE, that he employed the second best young programmer in town (Jeff Hove - my son Don is the best), and that I was willing to mediate the two companies.

So we formed a company, Lifease, Inc. The five founding principals were: Margaret, Adam, Warren, John Reiling, and me.

Margaret was an Registered Occupational Therapist (OTR) with a substantial history of work with elderly people and a national reputation. She had carried out a grant-funded project to develop her checklist and brought with her her company, Geriatric Environmental Concepts, from which our company bought the rights to the checklist. Adam was a free-lance marketing, public relations, and communications specialist. John was a health care executive, always busy, and a partner with Carl Christenson in an investment company, Carling, which was the major financial investor in Lifease. I ended up as the Board Secretary and the drafter of legal documents (subject to review by our legal firm, but usually not much modified).

I'll say only a little more about our corporation affairs, and concentrate on our technical and human operations.

Margaret, Adam, and I did a lot of work on the project before we officially began work on July 1, 1991. As usually happens I did most of the papers, such as drafting the business plan and licensing agreements and refining the proposed conceptual units and programming logic of EASE. Because I was away on an archaeological dig in Nebraska for the fist two weeks of our official operation, I came back to an office with furniture and a secretary, plus arrangements for consultants in Occupational Therapy (OT) and nursing.

I was the Systems Director, the person responsible for the conceptualization, logical structure, programming, and hardware of the EASE project. Consultation with Margaret and Adam and our consultants went into carrying out most of this. The programming was contracted to Emeritus, Warren's company, specifically to Jeff Hove, and I worked with him to retrieve some blocks of code from other programs we had worked on together. Jeff did the actual programming since I don't know how to do that. The software he used was PROGRESS, a kind of database manager and a fourth generation language. But I was responsible for integrating all the work, and I could overrule even Margaret (our CEO and Board President) on anything where I felt I had to dig in my heels.

Anyone interested in how our thinking developed as we created EASE can find it well documented in the numerous internal memos I wrote to consolidate our ideas. Maybe they still exist somewhere in my files.

We fairly rapidly worked out the conceptual structure of EASE. I proposed that we use, as our working unit, "Functions." These are sets of operations that a person has to carry out in order to "use" the home, and that are both possessed by the person and required by the home. This made it possible to describe the person and the home in the same terms. This is a crucial departure from usual clinical reasoning, where one set of concepts (the clinical status of the person) has to be compared to the set of concepts in which the demands of the home are stated.

My use of the "Functions" concept was almost instinctive. I had worked with critical vocational behaviors in a couple of my earlier incarnations and the basic proposition was the same: to use concepts that consist of large enough behavioral units to be fairly comprehensive without being too numerous, small enough to be trans-situational, critical to over-all effectiveness, and capable of reliable observation and scoring.

The casting of EASE in a logic frame that allows the person and the environment to be described in the same terms is a crucial feature of EASE and one that is unique among evaluation instruments as far as I know. I drew this feature from my background in psycho-vocational instrument design and in program evaluation. It allows the program to identify problems in an unambiguous manner: "A Problem is an instance where an Element of the home requires more of a given Function than the person has." Doing it this way overleaps the whole tedious business of relating clinical diagnoses of people with functional characteristics of the home. It also makes the instrument useable to any intelligent person, whether or not trained as an OT. Margaret didn't buy that but it's true.

Up to this point, the main approach in instrument design had been to describe the person in diagnostic terms (full hip replacement, or shoulder injury, or limited range of motion of elbow). This last is close to, but not the same as, our conceptualization of Functions. How does one relate these person-descriptors to the characteristics of the home? What are the practical implications? The answer is that the therapist has to use a clinical process, very hard to communicate, and beyond the capability of a computer.

What we came up with as Functions is operation-oriented. The Functions are units of what can be done (by the person) and what must be done (the home's demands), and the two can be compared directly.

Functions, in their own right, generate a most useful description of the person's abilities, in very practical terms. But they have a more important utility. Using the technique of discrepancy evaluation, Functions allows one to judge the home against the criteria set by the person. One does not judge the person as inadequate against the criteria of life; one judges the home as not appropriately usable by this particular person. The functional ability/demand feature of EASE creates, and is the linchpin of, a whole system of looking at person/environment interaction, seeing it as a system instead of as parts described in unrelated languages.

I contend that this way of looking at problems has very wide applicability. In particular, it could be applied to worker-workplace interaction in rehabilitation. If I were younger, and had a workplace such as a university to work from, I'd exploit that. Well, we all leave this world with unfinished business.

In Margaret's checklist there was the nucleus of a database of useful products, and she had a wide acquaintance with the sources of both clinical and everyday products. She had a whole library of catalogs, ranging from Sears to those health and craft-and-novelty catalogs we all get in our junk mail. It remained for us, and EASE, to systematize it.

Margaret assembled a group of Occupational Therapy (OT - remember?) students who would do some work for academic credit. We had one OT aspirant who had completed her course work and lacked only an internship to be certified (OTR - Registered Occupational Therapist). This was Shannon Hackett. Sharon also had keyboard skills, not to mention a lot of intelligence. I set her up with a simple database manager on our computer so that she could make a file of all the data being assembled. There was one file of product data, and one of data on the sources, and they were linked by code numbers generated by my program. These databases were not the EASE program, but they could be entered into any program that was written.

In addition to the data given in the catalogs I had Shannon enter a "generic name" for each product. The generic name was the common name by which a person would call the product if he didn't have the name that had been given by the supplier. For example, in addition to the catalog name "Acme unscrew-all," Shannon would enter the more descriptive name "Under-counter serrated jaw jar opener." This germ of an idea was to pay off later but at the time we didn't tumble to it.

The team of OT students went through the catalogs and marked any product that would be useful to a person with functional limitations. (Margaret had pre-marked many of the items, and she reviewed the choices as they were made.) The products ranged from the obvious grab bars to easily-handled kitchen utensils. Many items were common everyday: lever door handles, lighted keychains, cordless electric can openers. Others were at that time new on the market, such as lamps that could be switched by touching the base. Some items were quite specialized, such as spoons with swivel bowls. I had set up the database for automatic serial numbering and the number eventually passed 5,300. At that time we had no handy way to deal with duplications, so every duplication of product in more than one catalog meant a separate listing.

I posted charts of the logic and of the Functions and Elements as we identified and defined them. Margaret and other expert OTs did the identification and I wrote down the definitions. At that early date Margaret and the other OTs thought of me as a computer guru, and they had no real grasp of my grounding in rehabilitation, adaptive devices and instrument design, much less of what I could do to clarify and specify ideas. Fairly soon they were saying things in public (to defend my presence on this "professional" development project) as, "He is able to understand the ideas of OTs." As if this were something odd. They first tolerated me, then came to depend upon me for getting the ideas into form that could be used in a simple-minded computer. Sometimes, it took arguing.

As Systems Director I had to foresee the consequences throughout the EASE system of any component of the design and any change. As a result I sometimes had to argue against ideas that in themselves were great, but that would give us trouble down the road. That's one thing Systems Directors are for.

Anyhow, we came up with some 125 Functions, such as "Sit down to, and arise from, a seated position," and "Visual acuity (later changed to 'See clearly') at a distance of about 16 inches." Some of the Function constructs were pedestrian, such as "Lift foot over an obstacle," and some trod close to other professional turf, such as "Hear pure tones in the upper range." We got past the turf problems by keeping our definitions such that a lay person could observe and record - though we always reserved the judgment components of EASE to OTRs in the first years.

We also came up with some 110 Elements of the home, such as "Favorite chair," and "Stairs in the interior." This was to break the home into a feasible number of discrete focuses for observation of functional demand. Now we had the two halves of a system for identifying problems: the Functions in which the person and the home had complementary ability and demand; and the Elements in which demand could be observed.

I set up a system in which Margaret and other OTs could attribute functional demands to the home's Elements. Each attribution of a functional demand to an Element would constitute a Problem if, and only if, the Element demanded more of a Function than the person had. A person who had had an impairment was not a problem, nor was a demanding part of the environment a problem by itself.

I also structured a scoring system for the functional ability of the person and one for the functional demand posed by Elements, with the score systems being phrased in directly comparable terms. For example, in the Function "Sit down to, and arise from, a seated position," the person might have an ability in that Function at the level of "3. Can sit and rise with fixed handholds." An Element, the favorite chair, might pose the demand in this Function at a level of "5. Requires sitting and rising without handholds." Now we had two numerical scores of the same thing, one for the person and one for the environmental element. The computer could manage numbers, and it could store the information that this chair demanded a greater (5) amount of this Function than the person had. Behold: a computerizable instrument.

But that was not enough. We also had to find a way for the computer, when it found a problem, to look up appropriate solutions. It was like, and in fact I posted, the famous cartoon of the two professors at the chalkboard. The board is covered on one side with dense math equations, and on the other side with equally dense figures. In the middle there is a gap, with the words, "And then a miracle happens." One prof says to the other, "I think you ought to be more explicit about that second step." That was our situation. We had this gap between the two sides.

Side one: a Problem, that could be stated as "This person's favorite chair demands a greater ability in the sitting and rising Function than this person has." Side two: grab bars, chairs with better arms, and similar solutions -- buried among offset door hinges, jar openers, reachers of 225 kinds, etc. And in the middle a gap that a skilled professional could intuitively bridge (although ideosyncratically and fallibly), where a miracle had to be constructed in order for the computer to make the retrieval.

We solved it by brute strength. Margaret and other OTs specified, by serial number, the products that could solve each of the 1,700 potential problems.

I worked with Jeff Hove, our programmer, on the structure of the EASE program. This was easier than may appear. Jeff and I had worked on other things together for some 10 years, and we knew our mutual thinking. Jeff had a set of program code blocks from a related Emeritus project that could be adapted to EASE, and I had been a consultant on that project. Besides, Jeff has a broad conceptual grasp, and he was able to see the entire problem at one view. This was the only thing that allowed the two of us, who knew something about how long it takes to build software, to agree to the EASE project's insanely short time schedule.

I also attended to the matter of the hardware of EASE. We used laptop computers, then a fairly uncommon kind of machine, and I located printers that were also portable. I began to compose the EASE User's Manual.

We all worked like nailers during that summer and fall. Well, I had drafted out the basic logic earlier, but the official work hadn't begun until July of 1991.

Then, at the end of November, with my bow at full stretch, the bowstring broke.

I'd been out in a snowstorm on Halloween with granddaughters, wearing a Roman soldier costume with bare legs and arms. I came down with a back spasm that got worse over the next few days, and I spent all of December in bed. I kept in touch by phone, and Margaret or Adam came by once in a while, but essentially I was out of the picture until New Years. Then I was able to work part time for a month. During that time development of EASE went on. Some things were done that I would not have designed, such as a data-losing way to handle duplicate product listings, but by and large our basic program design was robust enough to become operational.

I don't think that any of the participants except Jeff, Warren and I had any idea of how miraculous it is that a large and novel computer program worked right out of the box. We had a working model of EASE that we could release for field testing *seven months* after we officially began work. Much of the credit for that should go to Jeff, who had to fill in on the conceptual work in my absence. Fortunately he had the control of the programming, so he could simply refuse to do some unwise things. It was still a miracle.

We trained a half dozen OTRs in how to use the EASE program, and we invested in the necessary hardware. Adam, the ever-resourceful Marketing Director, generated referrals and he structured the billing system. I'll skip here the details, but Adam is a skilled marketer. The OTs using EASE were contractors working under our authority, and the fee was to be paid to Lifease. It was a great idea and it worked - somewhat. It became evident that it wouldn't generate enough income to keep the company afloat. Over time the system wound down to a halt.

Meanwhile I was kept busy mending the inevitable flaws in EASE. It is a tribute to Jeff, among others, that the program never "blew up;" it never failed to work as designed. No user ever had the program quit or do logically weird things, or refuse to take orders. However it was far from perfect. I had deliberately designed it to be as simple as was consistent with doing its basic job. Over the years I had learned that a computer program that tries to be too complete in the beginning is not likely to work, and it is likely to be un-fixable. So EASE was, at its core, simple. However in making a simple program, it was also necessary to make it capable of accepting any reasonable added feature or contents, and that isn't a simple conceptual task. The basic framework was sound and it was capable of being elaborated almost infinitely.

So I worked with input from the users and with Lifease staff and Jeff to design additional features. With one exception (that matter of generic names of products I mentioned earlier), all the features that were added to EASE then and later had been accounted for in the basic program design.

Working out problems, collaborating with the others and drawing upon years of experience in related arenas occupied my time. I did a lot of technical writing, much of it for internal consumption. It was also my lot to do the project planning, such as timelines for the release of new versions and the steps that would have to be taken to meet the timelines.

We made a pretty good team. Margaret, with her extensive grounding in the clinical work that we were making explicit in a computer program, also contributed a very high level of intelligence in general. Adam, a creative man to begin with, could be depended upon to come up with new possibilities, and even to contribute to the substance of EASE. Jeff was able to not only do the programming needed, he was able to take a systems view that contributed to structure. Remember that it was Jeff who filled in for me during that month when I was in bed.

Our general office staff was Susan Smerz, who also showed a great deal of general capability. She became a bookkeeper as well as secretary. Three of our consultants, OTs named Sharon Stauffel, Barb Cochran, and Pat Watson, were integral workers in the development of EASE. They were especially helpful in choosing the vocabulary and in critiquing the applicability of EASE in the profession. Our consulting nurse, on the other hand, was not of much help (I think that she was hired to backstop me, because the others had been given no reason to think that I could contribute anything beyond "computerization.") And, of course, there was the yeoman service done by Shannon Hackett in building our database of products.

The next two years were simply an intense effort to make a sound product (EASE) better and more marketable. All of us worked on that. There were the usual concomitant professional things. I co-authored several papers with Margaret. In the beginning I relinquished any mention among the authors, since I had already made any professional mark I was likely to make. But when the time came when I actually did the full writing, then I asked for and got billing as senior author. But I'm not even bothering to add them to my vita, with one exception that I was working on at the time this chapter was drafted.

EASE came out in several versions. I attended to the software-hardware systems and to the records of who was using EASE. By now we were licensing its use to companies who paid us for the license and also paid us so much per use of the program. I milked the returned data disks for management and technical information. I wrote the license agreement and the general licensing conditions. Our attorney modified them only slightly. I responded to our licensees' technical inquiries and found that most of them were already covered in the manual I'd written for them. In the early years I also served as a general computer consultant to our licensees, but after 1994 we decided that we would restrict our technical support to EASE itself.

Our company ran on red ink. In mid-1993 we three principals on the staff (Margaret, Adam, and I) ceased to take salaries. Well, Adam, who was newly married, went on half pay for a while. Our deferred salaries continued to pile up on the books until we swapped them for stock options and stock warrants. The company got some cash infusion from the sale of stock to venture capitalists, and some loans. Jeff and I each bought $10,000 in stock. Margaret and Carl Christenson made unsecured loans to the company. And we tottered on.

We knew by mid-1994 that we had to replace Version 1 with a new version of EASE that would not need that fourth-generation language PROGRESS. As a new platform, we wanted a freestanding program in DOS and we wanted one that could be migrated to Windows eventually. Fortunately, Margaret's son Paul was available part time and we negotiated with him but didn't set to work on the new version immediately.

I had been writing working papers on the various subjects of EASE's future possibilities. At first they got the reaction of "That's nice. But let's deal with what we have to do now." I persisted and in due time was able to dust off the papers as the plans for an "EASE Two" developed. Anyone interested in the details can look up the dozen or so memos and design charts on the subject.

A new version gave rationale for a rebuilt database of products. I restructured the data elements in the light of our field experience and from time to time we got someone to work on it.

We also got a bit of money from the American Occupational Therapy Association. The project was to be a pictorial dictionary of useful devices. The product was to mostly be a book of pictures and names. Adam was one of the prime movers in initiating this project and of course Margaret had both the knowledge of what to include and the contacts in AOTA. The original target date was overly ambitious.

At any rate, Paul Christenson agreed to work on the new database of products as well as on the material for the pictorial dictionary in exchange for Lifease stock.

And now the subject of Generic Names revived. Remember that I said that we'd overlooked what later became an obvious way to make that miracle in the middle of the equation workable? As we discussed the names to give the objects to be pictured, it became obvious that we couldn't just give brand names. One object might have several brand names and the names wouldn't be descriptive. I had been working on the idea of Generic Names as the means to fix a design flaw (the data-wasting expedient that had been put in place while I was home in bed) and also to fix the flaw that I had introduced by not being explicit enough about what a generic name should be like when the data base was first set up.

Now I set to work in earnest on a taxonomy of generic names. It is not that others had not listed useful products; it was that the lists were not conceptually organized. They were lists, not taxonomies. There was neither inherent order nor a retrieval technique to them.

So I fell back on the time-honored nomenclature technique learned in the Army. It wasn't a "can opener thing you wear on your dogtag chain," it was a "can opener, twist operated, penetrating blade, with rim hook." A generic name identifies any item that it defines, a nomenclature names it from general-to-specific, and a taxonomy results from deriving all similar objects from the first term of the name. So I restated all 2700+ generic names that had been given to the products in our base on the basis of the related information in each product's record. I typed all of them personally. That was easier than trying to explain exactly what the rules were. In the early stages of this I didn't do all of it. We had a consultant, Mary Lee Cherney, OTR, and she constructed a good share of the names. But there is no substitute for a single editor so I reworked all of her output, too. In fact, over some months I refined the taxonomy by going over every line (the number had now grown to about 4200) and tinkering with the wording - at least eight complete runs through the list. Each run took some 20 hours of intense concentration, with the need to remember what was done to similar items.

The result of all this was a taxonomy in which you could distinguish a "Reacher, pistol grip, trigger operated, single vertical jaw" from a "Reacher, pistol grip, squeeze operated, single jaw." Why would anyone want to do that? because there were 250 kinds of reachers, and a person unable to move fingers independently should not be given a reacher that has a trigger operation. I attempted, mostly successfully, to make the terminology relevant to our Functions.

By the time all this was completed in late 1995 the first deadline for the pictorial dictionary had passed. The granting agency, AOTA, had contracted with an artist to make line drawings of the products we had selected to illustrate 300 key products, and the artist (a good one) had fallen out of the contract due to personal problems before the drawings were finished.

All was not lost. In the process of making the pictorial dictionary, the taxonomy of generic names had found a home in our new version of EASE. It solved, as I've said, the problem of the missing miracle step in our design. With our taxonomy we could now link problems to product solutions by means of the Generic Name. Instead of listing all the products that would solve a problem, we only had to specify one or more Generic Names, and the computer would find the appropriate products. And since the specific products and their data (source, catalog number, price, etc.) kept changing, we could simply give them each the proper Generic Name and the program would run without our having to make any other link.

There is an overlap of time here. In the middle of 1995, I retired from being an employee of Lifease and became a consultant working on a billing-for-work basis. The transition from employee to consultant was nearly imperceptible, because all of us on the staff were now spending much of our time on other matters.

Before I officially retired I had the satisfaction of seeing the long-expected Version II of EASE come out of Paul's work. He and Margaret and I had been working on that for some time. Version II was a great improvement, and not only because it used the mechanism of the Generic Names. It was faster, it looked better on the screen and on the printed reports, and the users were more satisfied with it. Its most successful market was with the colleges and universities that were using it as a teaching device for Occupational Therapists and Occupational Therapy Assistants.

I did my last work on EASE in the late 1990s. It wasn't much. EASE had gone a different route, due to the financial failure of the company and the shift to a one-person consulting effort by Margaret Christenson.

EASE as a program was truncated. It was adapted to use by Occupational Therapists only. This was the direction that its owner chose. My choice would have been to expand it into new fields, such as to vocational rehabilitation and into individualized architectural design. Ah well.

My time sheets for the next two years show intermittent work for the company. Forgive the details, but that's the only way I know how to tell you what I worked at.

The EASE program was undergoing a change into its next generation. I was still the word merchant and still the technical "expert."

I edited the file of Elements for review by Margaret, and edited and compiled her responses. I edited the files of Elements and Functions again, and wrote the new manual. (It was necessary to go over those things repeatedly in order to catch inconsistencies and to make sure that the verbal parts -- the definitions and scores -- were clear and precise and yet readable.) Then I test-ran the first version of the new EASE program, EASE2000, and worked with the programmer, Paul Christenson, on findings. I set up the program disks for a new user who showed promise of being a big customer and wrote the instructions for loading it.

When problems arose (and they always do, especially when a new program is used at a remote site) I diagnosed them and called or wrote to the users to correct them. I worked on the installation disks, the computer disks that were sent to new users to get their programs installed.

We were revising the linkages between the program and its database of products that were found in new editions of catalogs, so I set up the database program and instructed the part-time people who were entering the data, usually delivering the portable computers to them at their homes. I took their output and collated it into the data disks that the programmer could load into the EASE2000 master program.

I set up the portable computers that Margaret and Adam were taking to conferences to demonstrate our program.

I devised the linkage for sources of products that were to be found in local stores, not in catalogs, and connected the sources (such as "your local hardware store") to the generic product names.

I worked out and wrote down a new way of conceptualizing the function we had broadly defined as "Cognition." I continued for a while to manage the records of our contracts with users and revised the contract forms before we all realized that this had to be done in the office by someone who was there all the time.

Above all, I wrote. For the new program I wrote the content of the Help screens that the user would see while using the program. I re-wrote the entire User Manual again to conform to the new program interface, and prepared the materials for use in training conferences. And of course I continued to work on the logic of the program as its interface was changed and its capability was expanded.

Some of the tasks done in the next two years were brief, taking only an hour. Some of them were longer, such as the 31 hours I spent in three days to write the new Manual. My time tally ends in June, 1997 though by then a year had elapsed since I had done any billable work for the company and had not been paid for some months before that.

Meanwhile I worked quite a bit on a project that we had conceived earlier. Adam had made the first proposal and I had written out the plan of action to accomplish it. "It" was to be a book that would be a "pictorial dictionary" of products that are useful to people with impaired functions. For the many hours that this was to take I did not bill Lifease, doing it as an unpaid professional contribution.

There had been in circulation for years a Gadget Book. It was a set of drawings of items such as various buttonhooks and adapted eating utensils. It was a modest book, maybe 30 pages, but it was used by just about every Occupational Therapist as a sort of memory stimulus. It was also useful in describing to patients the products that were being prescribed. The Gadget Book was sponsored by the American Occupational Therapy Association, an organization in which Margaret was a prominent member, serving on various boards and committees. Adam's idea was to make a better, more systematic, more comprehensive and more useful book to replace the Gadget Book.

We had the raw materials. Over the years we had systematically searched out and described the products. We had worked out the generic names for the products and we had them on digital file. However, our file was a base in a computer program and not ready for publication.

I wrote out the plan of how to produce such a book, which we called The Pictorial Dictionary at that time. Margaret negotiated with the American Occupational Therapy Association (AOTA) for their sponsorship of the project. Her negotiations led to Lifease getting a grant to hire help and the AOTA's promise to be the publisher.

I mentioned earlier that some work was done on the Pictorial Dictionary while I was still theoretically an employee of Lifease. We carried over the terminology from EASE and to save keystrokes here I'll refer to the Generic Names as "GNs." We started with a list that I'd given occasional attention to over the years and that was somewhat systematic.

I wrote out the conceptual structure of a proper GN: as many as four terms, the first term being the most general and the most nominative; as many as three additional terms, in decreasing order of generality; and the GN being the statement of a *type* of product, not the name given by a supplier.

For example, a supplier might sell an "Acme reacher," while the GN that describes all reachers of that type might be "Reacher, pistol grip, trigger operated, vertical jaw." Incidentally, it turned out that we had to use over 100 GNs to describe all the reachers on the market.

The Reacher example also illustrates another of our specifications of a proper GN: the GN should focus on the functional aspects of the product. The example illustrates functionality in that this generic reacher is of a kind can be held by a person who can grasp the (pistol) grip in the hand, and can squeeze with one finger as opposed to squeezing the entire hand; and its business end is one that goes up and down, not side to side. This remarkably simple conceptual scheme was, surprisingly, new and had to be sold. The conceptualizer quickly learns that what is obvious to him is not obvious to anyone else.

But there is no substitute in editing for a single editor. I ended up re-doing the list completely at least eight times over the next couple of years. The list eventually was settled upon as comprising about 5,300 GNs, so going over each one eight times was a large job. Each pass through the list took about two days. Although I didn't keep a formal time tally my estimate is that I spent well over 500 hours on the project before it was completed.

So we had a list of some 5,300 GNs. Now to make it pictorial.

Margaret, Adam and I spent some time going through catalogs to find illustrations of GNs. The agreement with AOTA was that we could supply 400 pictures. They would give the pictures to an artist whom they would hire, who would make line drawings that stressed the functional characteristics of the products. We selected the pictures from catalogs, pasted them to backing, and I printed and attached appropriate GNs. We sent off the box.

Some time passed, and we received a few pictures. They looked OK to me, not excellent but passable, and I sent them back with my approval. Then there came a time when we didn't receive any pictures, and the deadline for publication became unrealistic. I wrote and called AOTA, but didn't get much attention, presumably because I'm not an Occupational Therapist. (Throughout this project, I had a hard time getting my AOTA editor to correspond directly to me, the senior author. AOTA depended upon a sort of old-girls' network, of which Margaret is a member, and Margaret didn't always know what I wanted and didn't always tell me what she had learned.) Margaret called her friends in AOTA and we were told that the artist had had medical problems and would not be able to continue. They would get another artist. We began to get pictures again. They were stiff and clearly computer-generated but by a program that wasn't state of the art. Perhaps unwisely, I considered them to be passable and OKd them.

Then we had enough pictures to review, fewer than we had expected by now, but enough to sample. Margaret, Adam and I sat down to review them. Adam, who is the one with graphic experience, said that they simply would not do, and I had to agree. So I had the job of telling my contact editor at AOTA that we would have to get our own artist locally. AOTA agreed and Adam found an artist who would do the drawings for $10 each, a very low price. The artist, Jeff Felson, made some samples which turned out to be vastly better than any we'd had from the AOTA artist, and AOTA agreed to fund the work.

In short order the pictures were completed and approved. Meanwhile, I was writing the short text for the book and getting the GNs into final form. I wrote a glossary too, together with the odd bits of information that publishers need to complete a book. The AOTA editor was now corresponding directly with me, and it looked like we could get the book published in time for the annual meeting of AOTA in April, 1998.

There were some final glitches, as there always are. When the book was at last off the press, and when I didn't receive my promised advance copy or even a photocopy of its title page as requested, Margaret again activated the old girls' network with AOTA and the book was shipped. I received my copy on 2/20/98. It has a well-designed cover, 300 illustrations, 5,300 GNs, a large glossary, and 177 pages. Nearly half the book is dense text listing those GNs. Altogether a worthy publication to be the first and last formally published book citing me as senior author.

Did I say "worthy"? Yes and no. As a freestanding publication it is liable to the charge that it "doesn't do anything." That's a reasonable charge against any dictionary or list. To make our book useful, more needs to be done with it.

My proposal was to make a companion program that contained the set of names as a database and that linked each Generic Name to the source(s) where the product can be obtained. The first version would be in a computerized random retrieval program. In the future the dictionary could be put onto compact disk with pictures as well as text. Both of these versions have been rejected so far on the grounds that they would conflict with and possibly hurt the sales of our main product. I also think that they were understood as the limited idea that they would add nothing except random searchability to the book. The first objection is tempered in my mind with the fact that Lifease has virtually abandoned the EASE program except for use in colleges and universities, so there isn't much to conflict with. My bet is that there is a ready market for a resource like the GN-source linkage and that market would give Lifease an income that it doesn't now have.

As matters now stand with our flagship program, it is not generating significant revenue. It is not much used in the field mostly because third-party funders of health programs want a quicker, if dirtier, use of OT. The funders don't pay for this kind of diagnostic work by OTs. Colleges and universities do value and use the program to teach its kind of clinical reasoning to OT students, but they don't pay enough for it to more than break even with our current cost of production. That doesn't recoup our development cost.

In late 1998 came the request to merge the Functions of EASE into a smaller set of super-functions, and to write them and their definitions. This I did in a matter of a few hours. That work went into a new product that is being marketed through an existing national catalog of aids and similar. The market may be there.

By the year 2000 the outlook for Lifease was limited. Some of its products may take off and create income. My financial, time, and emotional investments are set on "hold" until something happens. I don't expect to recoup anything from my investments. If I don't, it still was a great ride.

RETIREMENT II AND WRITING
1995 or so to 2009

I entered upon my second retirement at the beginning of September, 1995. I was no longer an employee of Lifease or any employee at all, a not unfamiliar situation, but this time it was one that felt pretty final.

I had lost my good wife Bernice in 1988. In 1995 I gained another good wife Ruth. At this writing I have 17 grandchildren (combining mine and Ruth's) and one great-grandchild. Being Grandpa and having a combined set of small pensions that add up to full support should be enough. But of course it isn't.

One night, about 3 AM, I lay awake thinking about Shamgar, one of the Judges of ancient Israel. All we are told about him is "After [the previous Judge] ruled Shamgar, who slew 600 Philistines with an ox goad. He also judged Israel." Here was a man with at least one great achievement about whom we knew nothing else. It didn't seem fair. So I got up and wrote a short fictional autobiography or memoir for Shamgar, trying to do him justice.

Well and good. But such things don't stop there. It then became incumbent to do the same for the 19 other characters in the Book of Judges. That went on for some months and a book was born.

I'd written other book-length screeds, notably "What Did You Do in the War, Daddy?" and "What Did You Do for a Living, Daddy? (the draft for this book)" And a few travel journals of considerable length. I seem to be compelled to write.

After the fictional memoirs of the Judges characters were finished it felt natural to go on to a fictional autobiography of the Judge and Prophet Samuel. So that got done.

Rather than let the manuscripts languish I decided to self-publish them. Duplicating them and binding them with the facilities offered by local firms like Office Max taught me that it cost about $12 to make each copy in 8½ X11 format and with decent binding. That would never do. Then I found that there are printing firms that cater to self-publishers. I settled on Lulu.com.

Like other such firms, Lulu.com will print for you but you're on your own as to editing and proofreading and creating cover art. And there's no editor to tell you that your book isn't worth printing. There's no copyreader to tell you about your misspellings or other mistakes, or if your pages are out of order. But self-publishing firms do (for a fee) get you an ISBN, the International Serial Book Number that is needed for protecting publishing rights, and they get you listed in the book trade, and they do produce nice-looking paperback books at a reasonable cost. "Reasonable" here means about $7.50 for books like "Judges" and "Samuel" and a bit over $8.00 for this one.

After the historical fiction works on the Judges and Samuel I also wrote a straightforward book of the history of that period. So far, that means that I've published the Judges Trilogy ("Judges, Rulers and One Angry Levite," "Samuel, Seer" and "The Times of the Judges") plus "What Did You Do in the War, Daddy?" renamed "Ordinary GI." So far the Judges Trilogy is selling moderately and "Ordinary GI" is on Alibris.com, probably put there by the printer. Currently I'm working on the same blend of fiction and history as the Judges Trilogy to cover the Time Between the Testaments. If God gives me inspiration and years.

CLOSURE, SORT OF
1009

With the shipment of my archives off to the National Rehabilitation Association and to other depositories, some sort of closure seems to be appropriate on a career that I've always identified as "rehabilitation psychologist."

I've been off the line for many years and enjoy the mid-eighties. Retirement is pleasant. My health, thank God, is good -- with the help of senior chemicals and a synchronizing heart pacemaker. I no longer fret about what is happening in the fields I no longer participate in, I just lay back and enjoy what I hear of them.

All my life, people have been good to me, and they continue to do that.

Who knows what comes next, if anything in this life? None of us knows. So, one sunrise at a time. Sunrise is good.

Peace.

Your Notes

www.ingramcontent.com/pod-product-compliance
Lightning Source LLC
Chambersburg PA
CBHW030503260626
47157CB00005B/1631